The File On
John Ormond

To East Dover Folk
Enjoy!

March 2022

D1264013

The File On John Ormond

An Inspector Mason Mystery

J.D. Mallinson

To order additional copies of this book, contact:
Xlibris Corporation
1-888-795-4274
www.Xlibris.com
Orders@Xlibris.com

37134

For Peter, Judy, Anne and Geoffrey

CHAPTER ONE

JOHN ORMOND DIS-
APPEARED around the
end of April, 1980. A small notice in the personal column of
Helsingin Sanomat, the main Finnish broadsheet, some weeks
later recorded the fact, read by but affecting little the daily
lives of the half-million or so inhabitants of the Baltic capital.
Subsequent enquiries produced no hard information, and
although the city police continued their investigations on and
off during the summer months to pacify the British Embassy,
they reluctantly felt obliged to shelve the case. Ormond, in so
far as anyone was aware, had few immediate family; yet there
had been sporadic interest on the part of the British press,
and some unusual features of the case aroused the interest of
Scotland Yard. They dispatched a senior member of Special
Branch who was experienced in foreign assignments, to see if
he could come up with some new leads.

It was already late-November by the time Inspector George
Mason arrived unannounced in Helsinki, just the time of year
when winter was beginning to bite. As yet there had been little
snow, but temperatures were well down towards zero and a

strong wind blew across the eastern Baltic bearing damp, chill air with it. George Mason cursed his luck as he walked the short distance from his hotel to Police Headquarters facing the South Harbor. He possessed a smattering of Finnish from a semester he had once spent as an exchange student at Tampere University; hence his selection for this assignment. At any other time of year he would have relished it; yet just as he had been finalizing plans to go to Italy with his wife Adele on a skiing trip—another postponed vacation—he had been put on short notice for a visit to Helsinki. Ormond possessed sensitive material of some kind and it was up to him to discover what that was. With a fair bit of luck, the whole business might be cleared up in a couple of weeks and he would get his vacation in after all. His wife Adele was keenly looking forward to it. If, on the other hand, his preliminary enquiries came up with nothing, the case might simply be abandoned; filed away under the heading UNSOLVED.

As he strode along the tree-lined boulevard, briskly to create the pretence of warmth, he glanced up apprehensively at the hostile sky. The benches in the park, littered with leaves, had long-since been abandoned, the gravel paths deserted save for the odd squirrel foraging for beechnuts. The inhabitants of Helsinki, their faces taut and pale beneath Pushkin hats, paid him little heed as they hurried by. Molded by the elements, they were an inward race difficult to get to know well; unlike the out-going Italians he had met in the Dolomites. Key Finnish qualities, he mused, were more about endurance, fortitude, economy of words. What a brave showing they had made against the Russian army on the eastern front. A plucky little nation, the Finns. One could not help but admire them.

The local police may not be of much help, he mused, entering beneath the arched lintel of Police Headquarters, whose tall windows looked out unhindered towards the open bay, empty of shipping save for a few yachts waiting to be removed before the sea froze. His interview with Major Viljo Forsenius was scheduled for 11 am. From his name, Mason judged that he was a Swedo-Finn, a member of an ethnic minority whose first language was Swedish; for that reason he probably spoke good English, which was much closer to it than it was to Finnish. With Forsenius in the large, modern office was Ronald Ryle, an official of the British Embassy, who rose from his chair to greet him.

"Very grateful that you came out so readily," he said. "The ambassador has been much embarrassed by the unexplained disappearance of a British national."

"But the Ormond case was shelved months ago by the city police, wasn't it?" Mason asked, with a pointed glance at the major, a dapper figure in a dark-blue uniform.

"The British press has been taking renewed interest in the case," Ryle explained. "Seems that Ormond has an elderly aunt living in Macclesfield, his only living relative. Contacted her local newspaper and also her MP."

"As far as we ourselves are concerned," Forsenius said, "this case is officially closed. But we are quite willing, at the behest of the British Embassy, to place our file at your disposal and provide any back-up you may require."

He nodded deferentially towards Ryle, who sat with legs crossed and hands tautly clasped at the knee. He then reached inside a drawer and drew out a buff-colored folder with the name JOHN ORMOND inscribed on the cover. He also produced a pocket-diary which the *talomies*, the manager of the apartment block where Ormond lived, had come across quite recently and handed in.

"The ambassador is most anxious that this affair be cleared up as soon as possible," Ryle said. "My office will provide any assistance you may need in the way of translation or interpreting."

Mason seemed not to have heard the remark. Examining the pocket-diary for a brief moment, he placed it in his side pocket. The buff folder he put in his briefcase.

"Mr Ryle," he said. "We must all be patient. Police enquiries take time."

"I'm sure he understands that perfectly," Forsenius remarked.

The brief interview concluded, Mason and Ryle left together. Once outside, the latter became much more affable, mentioning that the detective would be very welcome at Embassy social functions. That was, if he could spare the time. They parted on cordial terms and Mason began walking back towards the city center, declining the offer of a lift in Ryle's official car. He crossed the tram-lined square to take a closer look at the harbor. The bay spread out towards the Gulf of Finland, where freighters were headed to the Baltic ports farther south. A huge crane was parked on the quay, waiting for ships to arrive, and there were signs of an early-morning market, bits of discarded vegetables and scraps of fish the gulls were eagerly snapping up. Turning to walk along the tree-lined Esplanade, he admired the elegance of these official waterfront buildings conceived in Empire style and finished in pale, pastel stucco: ochres, pinks and light-blues. Behind them was the imposing Lutheran Cathedral, keeping a watchful, one might almost say a paternal, eye on the scene.

A short walk brought him to the end of Esplanade, where it joined Mannerheim, the city's main thoroughfare, near a large circular building. It was a theater, judging from the posters on the wall. They were playing Strindberg. Across from the theater was a spacious mezzanine restaurant whose picture windows looked down on the busy scene. Mason decided to grab an early lunch and peruse the information Forsenius had just given him in the warm interior of The Three Counts. It was a self-service establishment, obviating the problem of deciphering menus in Finnish. He chose a dish that looked like pork, but it had more the texture of beef. Either reindeer or elk, he decided, both of which were common dishes here, according to the guidebook he had bought at Seutola Airport that very morning. Served with mashed potatoes and red whortleberries, it was a delicious, warming meal for a cold day.

He was still sitting there after the lunch-hour trade had peaked, nursing his third cup of coffee. His fellow diners and their lively, incomprehensible conversations in the vernacular had nearly all departed and he was left in undistracted speculation on the fate of his missing compatriot. He hardly knew where to begin. Only an awareness that he had been in similar predicaments before and generally won through in the end encouraged him. He had a strange suspicion, however, that this time his luck might be out. His presence in Helsinki at all he regarded more or less as a formality, one of those face-saving operations mounted to satisfy officialdom. The local police were obviously completely stumped.

He took out the buff folder and examined it closely. It listed the known facts about John Ormond. Place of birth: Coventry. Profession: translator, retained on a free-lance basis by the Polyglot Institute, Mikonkatu. Status: single. Of medium height, with blond hair and blue-gray eyes. Address: Apartment 6C, Strandweg 125, Kulosaari, Helsinki. The word *saari* was Finnish for 'island', so he had evidently lived on one of the larger, inhabited islands of the archipelago. *Katu* was the word for 'street'. Mikonkatu, he discovered from his city map, was quite central, near the main railway station, a noted piece of architecture designed by Saarinen. He would soon pay it a visit.

He replaced the folder in his briefcase with a shrug. There was certainly something very odd about this whole affair. An Englishman vanishing without trace from one of the most law-abiding of cities. Suicide could probably be ruled out, he considered. Enterprising young men—and who could doubt that Ormond was just that?—were not in the habit of taking their own lives, either for financial or romantic reasons. A free-lance translator's livelihood might be more precarious than some, but in a country so dependent on foreign trade as Finland there should be no shortage of well-paid work. The one curious fact Mason did unearth was a discrepancy in dates.

Ormond supposedly disappeared around April 30th, when he failed to report for work. But he was last seen alive, according to Forsenius, on the 23rd, fully seven days earlier. Somewhere in that interval lay the clue to his puzzling fate. He penned a postcard to Adele, complaining about the weather on the back of a view of snowbound Lapland and mentioning his recent purchase of warm clothing to forestall her reminder, before heaving his portly frame from the table. Remembering that he had already paid for his meal on entering, he descended the short flight of stairs to street-level.

CHAPTER TWO

MASON SOON LOCATED the address of the Polyglot Institute in Mikonkatu. It was an old building with a creaking wooden staircase leading up to the second-floor accommodation of the language school. As he approached, he could hear the sound of English lessons in progress. He rapped on the glass-paneled door, which was opened after a few moments by a tall, angular blonde. Explaining his errand, he was shown into the private office of the proprietor, Arthur Greenwood, a fifty-something Englishman.

"John Ormond?" he enquired, in some surprise. "You are investigating his case?"

"I understand he was employed here as a translator," Mason said.

"That is correct," Greenwood replied, offering him a chair. "We are mainly a teaching institute, but some of our students bring in translation work from their employers, mainly firms engaged in import and export."

"What was Ormond working on when he failed to show up at the end of April?" To the detective's mind, there might be a useful connection.

"The city police have already been through all that months ago," Greenwood said, petulantly. "But if you insist, it was a contract drawn up by a prominent coffee importer."

Just then, the telephone rang. Mason waited patiently for him to finish, contemplating with some annoyance the tide-mark of damp rising up the instep of his leather shoes. The walk from The Three Counts had nearly ruined them and he would have to invest in a sturdier pair. He listened intrigued to the strange babble of sound. Greenwood spoke fluent Finnish, indicating that he had probably lived in Finland for several years. When he replaced the receiver, he glanced up in mock-surprise to see Mason still sitting there.

Just the re-arrangement of a lesson," he explained. "Is there something else you wish to know? It's all very baffling."

"Tell me," Mason said, with studied lack of haste and a certain irony, "if I'm not taking up too much of your time . . ."

Greenwood was sorting papers on his desk, officiously.

"Is there some sort of English community here; somewhere expatriates might meet after working hours. A club, say . . . or a bar?"

"There are several points of contact, in fact," the proprietor replied, resigning himself to the other's presence. The English Church, for example; the Marlowe Club, a dramatic society that puts on English and American plays; occasional events, such as the Queen's Birthday at the embassy. And we arrange various cultural events here at the institute. Lectures on subjects like heraldry, for example. Expatriates sometimes contribute."

"Was Ormond involved in these activities?"

"To a certain extent," Greenwood replied. "I never met him at the English Church, St. George's. But he did sometimes drop in at the Marlowe."

"How often would that be?"

Greenwood reflected. "Once or twice a month, perhaps. He was not what I would call a good mixer. Seemed to prefer the society of his Finnish friends, though I never met any of them personally."

"But he did use the Marlowe Club."

"Everyone needs the company of his fellow-countrymen from time to time," Greenwood said, for the first time betraying a streak of sympathy. "John Ormond was no exception. He would drop in, order a drink or two and pass the time of day."

"With anyone in particular?"

"With the club steward, mainly. They were from the same city. Birmingham, I think it was. No, it was Coventry."

"And the steward's name?" Mason asked.

"Ellison. Grant Ellison, a man considerably older than John; a sort of father-figure."

"Did Ormond have any enemies, in so far as you were aware?"

"Don't we all, Inspector?" Greenwod replied, cryptically.

"What I mean is: were there any marked animosities within the English community?"

"Likes and dislikes, certainly. Nothing I would describe as animosity, no. We're much too close-knit a community for that. Not all that many of us, after all."

"But Ormond himself was not particularly close-knit, you implied. An odd man out, so to speak?"

"That's right," said Greenwood. "But entirely of his own choosing. Expatriates are sometimes like that. They cultivate their friendships mainly among the native community. Seen it happen several times."

"Female acquaintances?" Mason prompted.

"Possibly," replied the other, more amiably.

Mason rose and smoothed down the front of his fur-lined coat, which stuck out awkwardly because it was new.

"Thank you for your time," he said, offering a heavy palm.

"Glad to be of help, Inspector," Greenwood said, as Mason was leaving. "And by the way, I should be glad to hear of any developments."

Mason nodded curtly, but said nothing. He was thinking about footwear.

In the shoe department of the same store he had visited that morning he took out the pocket-diary and re-examined it. It listed only a handful of names and telephone numbers, but no addresses. What a stroke of luck it had turned up at all; it gave him a bit more to go off than the city police had had. He formed the impression that this would be a quite lengthy enquiry, following up all possible leads. A pity he had not brought his skis, he mused, as the assistant scurried off to find a larger size of fur-lined boots and he was left gazing apprehensively at the heavy snow falling past the window.

Having asked the store assistant for directions to Kulosaari, he discovered that it was reached by a modern dual-carriageway wide enough to include parallel tramlines. He leaned forward eagerly in his seat as the powerful vehicle left the city center and suddenly accelerated across the bridge over the open bay. In another month or so the city's ports would be locked in winter ice, navigable only by ice-breakers. For now the freighters still plied slowly beneath the high suspension bridge, on their way to and from the old Hansa ports carrying mainly timber, the green gold on which the country's economy was based. Kulosaari, the island suburb, lay just beyond the bridge.

Ormond had chosen well, he reflected, as he alighted from the tram and commenced walking along the pine-fringed road towards secluded tenements with a seaward view. Strandweg 125 was a detached timber building of three floors, apparently a former private dwelling converted into apartments to accommodate a pressing population. Housing was at a premium in a capital city drawing an influx of migrants from rural areas, to help man more modern industries, and rentals were high. Kulosaari seemed to Mason one of the more prosperous areas. Ormond, he considered, must have been doing quite well as a translator to be living here, where Volvos and Mercedes stood in driveways, amid other unmistakable signs of affluence.

The *talomies* was not particularly helpful, but he did offer to open the relevant apartment, a small suite of rooms facing south across the open sea. He wondered if Ormond had chosen it specially for the view, and whether that implied a romantic side to his nature. It was indeed small, comprising a bed-sitter and adjoining bathroom, but no kitchen. He revised downwards his estimation of the translator's means. It was a good neighborhood, but the most basic level of accommodation. Did he supplement his regular income by less legitimate means? He may well have got mixed up in something, for all Mason knew, as he gazed beyond the window towards the Gulf of Finland, wondering if that had been the direction of his disappearance. Due south stood Tallinn, the capital of Estonia; due east was Leningrad, both of them inscrutable cities under totalitarian regimes. If Ormond was across that water, Mason realized there was little he could do to help him.

The *talomies*, a taciturn Finn nearing retirement, remained in the open doorway, as if expecting only a short visit.

"I trust everything is in order," he remarked, rather testily. "Major Forsenius said it would be in order to re-let. Accommodation like this is at a premium just now."

"I can well believe it," Mason said, moving to the bookshelves to examine the contents.

There were some interesting titles: novels in French by Sartre and Camus; Penguin paperbacks of modern English writers; some ski manuals; a Finnish/English dictionary and an older Russian/English one, used no doubt in his trade as a translator. Mason grimaced. French authors left him cold; they always had some ax to grind, some *ism* to promote. That Ormond read Jean-Paul Sartre, a leading exponent of the left, might mean something in itself.

The *talomies* was still standing motionless, hawk-like, in the doorway.

"I'll be down shortly," Mason said. "No need to wait about."

The man shrugged sullenly and left, making slow, heavy footfalls on the wooden stairway.

Mason took a closer look at the books, eventually selecting one with an unusual binding. It turned out to be a Russian novel, perhaps unavailable in local bookshops. On opening it, he noticed an inscription on the fly-leaf, written in Russian, of which he could decipher only the name 'Maxim' and a date.

As he quit the apartment and went downstairs, slipping the novel in his pocket to check if it was indeed unavailable in local bookshops, he thought it might be of some significance that it had come into Ormond's possession shortly before his sudden disappearance. And who was Maxim? It crossed his mind that the translator might have gone over to the other side. Harrington had mentioned sensitive information. If Ormond had defected with it, it would be one in the eye for Ryle and the Embassy people. The translator was evidently Russophile to some degree. He could also read the language and was acquainted with at least one Russian national, supporting Greenwood's view that he cultivated friendships outside the expatriate community. But did that make him a communist?

The *talomies* was hovering in the stairwell, a screwdriver in his hand, but evidently more interested in his unusual visitor than in property maintenance.

"When did you last see Mr Ormond?" Mason asked of him.

The man took a step back, prepared to say as little as possible, as if complying with instructions.

"I told Major Forsenius everything I know," he said. "There is nothing to add."

"Come now," Mason urged. "No need to be coy with me. I have the major's full authority and support."

"It is already six months ago. I do not recall when I saw him last. In any event, we seldom met. He was scarcely ever in his apartment, except to sleep."

"Was he here during the last week in April?"

"That particular week I was visiting my sister in Porvoo. She is old and infirm and needs help with the gardening and the household chores."

"Forsenius told me that you had visitors late one night, who went through Ormond's things."

"There were two of them," the other replied, matter-of-factly.

"You saw their faces?"

"One of them had a beard. That's all I remember about them."

"Were they both Finns?"

"One spoke Finnish, the clean-shaven one. I should say the other man was not Finnish. Finns hardly ever grow beards."

"How long did they stay?

"About half an hour. They made a mess of the place. I cleaned up after them and rang the police."

"Did they threaten you in any way?"

"No. But their attitude was menacing. They seemed intent on finding something up there. I have no idea what it was, or whether they were successful. They pushed past me without a word on their way out and sped off in a car towards the city center."

"You could not have prevented them?"

"They were not to be trifled with. I am nearly seventy years old."

"What will happen to Ormond's belongings now, if you re-let?"

"Major Forsenius is arranging for them to be stored at a police facility. Then I will list the apartment with an agency. We have already lost several months' rent."

"Then good luck," Mason said. "And thanks."

"*Nakemiin*," returned the other. "Au revoir."

CHAPTER THREE

THOUGHTS OF A skiing trip to Italy were receding from his mind as George Mason trudged the length of Alexanderinkatu in heavy snow towards the Music Exchange. *Directory Enquiries* had checked out for him the phone number which headed the short list on the first page of Ormond's pocket-diary. He had a hunch that this number held a particular significance since it had been inked over heavily and stood out boldly from the rest. Beside it was the name Helvi, an appropriately melodious name, he thought, for an employee of a music store. With luck, the girl still worked there; failing that, he should be able to obtain information as to her present whereabouts. Conscious that shops and stores closed their doors at 4 pm, and following his time-consuming excursion to the suburbs, he increased his gait.

He made it just in time. Fortunately, there were still customers inside hovering round the recordings and sheet-music shelves, postponing their purchases until the last minute, or simply browsing. He mixed with them, subdued his labored breathing and regained his composure. The swell of symphonic music, something by Sibelius, filled the store. He moved closer to the racks near the counter, where two young women were putting seasonal wrapping on purchases, and noted with a quickening of the pulse the name HELVI KILPINEN on one of the name-cards. While thinking up a ruse to speak with her privately, he glanced through the instrumental section, lighting on a Mozart violin concerto that was a particular favorite of Adele's. Noting soloist and conductor, he considered buying it as a Christmas gift.

Spotting a vacant booth in the far corner of the store, he took the recording to her, observing her closely as she placed it on the turntable. She conformed to national type, with high cheek bones, ash-blond hair and distant pale-blue eyes. Of medium height, her trim figure was offset by a cream-colored blouse and dark skirt. She seemed the sort of girl one might pass a score of times on an afternoon stroll down Mannerheim; yet she was no less an individual on that account.

She caught him staring and looked questioningly at him.

"The listening-booth is over there," she said, gesturing with her free hand.

He quickly entered it and listened for a few moments to the opening bars. The hand of the wall-clock showed 3.56 pm. In a few minutes the store would close for the day. Turning the volume down, he pressed the help button. Helvi, with a thinly-veiled look of annoyance, glanced over, then quit her post at the counter and walked across.

"It's closing time," she said. "Do you wish to buy the recording?"

"Don't be alarmed," he said. "I'm here regarding John Ormond."

"John!" she exclaimed, in amazement. "But who on earth are you? What is this, some kind of joke? I thought . . ."

He peered carefully into her startled eyes, now only inches from his own, for any tell-tale expression that betrayed something more than surprise. He saw nothing.

"What did you think, Miss Kilpinen?" he asked, quickly.

The girl took a step back and looked at him suspiciously. But her curiosity was roused.

"I thought that he might just possibly have gone back to England," she replied.

Mason shook his head. "No, that is not the case," he said. "John Ormond vanished, right here in Helsinki. About six months ago."

"You are from the police, aren't you?" she then said. "And you are saying something has happened to him."

The detective nodded gravely. "I need your assistance," he said, urgently.

"How can I possibly . . . ?"

It was now just turned 4 pm and the last customers were leaving the store. Helvi's colleague was closing her till.

"Is there somewhere we can talk?" he asked.

Helvi led the way back to the counter and wrote her address on a slip of paper.

"Come this evening after seven. It's by the Brunnspark. Take the Number 3 tram."

"I'll find it," he replied. "And you may wrap this recording in that elegant Christmas wrapping you have there."

Helvi smiled and did as she was bid. Watching her nimble fingers at work and her look of concentration, he found himself approving of Ormond's taste in women, feeling for the first time an almost personal interest in his fate. He also felt more confident now that he had taken some positive steps. Helvi could probably throw some light on Ormond's movements prior to his disappearance.

"See you at seven," he said, accepting the package and leaving the store.

Night had already closed in and the temperature had fallen sharply. It was impossible to remain long out of doors, yet the prospect of killing time in his small hotel room did not appeal to him. He tried a nearby cinema, but the show did not start until six. It would be difficult at this hour to get even a glass of beer, so strict were the local licensing laws, so he made his way through the snow to The Three Counts, where he had earlier taken lunch.

Trade was slack at this hour. Only a handful of customers sat at the polished tables drinking coffee and reading newspapers. He stopped in his tracks as he turned from the self-service counter and made towards a window seat, with the idea of observing the rush-hour bustle along the main street. The gentleman sitting over by the far wall struck him as vaguely familiar. He looked hard at him, but couldn't place the face. It was only when he had sat down with his drink and a newspaper that something registered in his mind. The man conformed to the mental picture furnished by the *talomies* of one of the intruders at the Kulosaari apartment. The strangely coincidental apparition, in the shape of a broad-faced, athletic-looking man with a fullish beard just then glanced up and looked past him, almost through him, with unwavering gaze. Mason dismissed the possibility as a thousand-to-one chance and settled down to browse through his paper. From time to time he glanced across the room in the man's direction, making careful note of his features in case their paths crossed again. This was the first person sporting a beard that he had encountered since his arrival in Finland.

Lacking sufficient knowledge of Finnish to tackle even the shorter articles, he limited his efforts to deciphering the captions beneath the photographs. A picture on the inside pages soon caught his eye, but he was distracted momentarily by the screech of brakes in the street below. Glancing down, he saw that a motorist had fallen foul of the tramlines. There was a prolonged sounding of the tram's horn, but no actual collision; a near thing, probably occurring often in this weather. The photograph. It showed the Russian author, Timor Tarkov, bearded and also bespectacled, looking straight at the camera with searching eyes. He concentrated hard on the wording of the caption, concluding that Tarkov had defected in the spring of that year and was now living in Switzerland.

On sudden impulse, he took out Ormond's pocket-diary and again went over all the entries. The name Maxim was recorded on two different dates during April, but without any reference to the full identity or whereabouts of that individual; not even a telephone number. It seemed a long shot, but also just possible that there might be some connection between Maxim, a translator who knew Russian and a defecting author who might well have come through Finland on his way south. Filing the impression in the back of his mind, he returned to the counter to buy one of the delicious open sandwiches they regularly served. The bearded man brushed past him as he did so, on his way out. Mason returned to his table and continued perusing the newspaper while savoring an egg-and-anchovy open sandwich with some fresh coffee. The restaurant gradually filled with people dropping in after work, striking lively conversations in Finnish that were like music to Mason's ears in that they represented normal social intercourse, friendships, confidences and trust. It was a kind of vicarious companionship.

"So you managed to find me," Helvi said, opening the door of a second-floor apartment in the well-heeled Brunnspark area of the city. The warm glow of the interior flowed out to greet him as the girl, attractively clad in a gray woolen dress, smilingly invited him in. She struck him as more relaxed, as if she had dismissed her initial suspicions. Whatever emotion she felt on Ormond's account, she betrayed none of it to him. The Finns were an introvert people, keeping their feelings largely to themselves.

"You shouldn't have taken the trouble," he protested, at her offer of coffee and *pulla*, a sort of cake invariably served with it. At her bidding, he eased his portly frame onto the deep sofa and surveyed the large apartment, his eye drawn magnetically to an easel by the window.

"You're an artist?" he remarked, approvingly.

Helvi seemed flattered, but shook her head as she stooped to fill his cup. Mason declined cream and sugar on account of his weight.

"A student of art would be more accurate," she replied.

"And the job at the Music Exchange?"

"Just to help with expenses. Not that I don't like it there. The hours are flexible, leaving me time to attend courses at the Academy."

"Do you mind if I take a look?"

He was only pretending to be an art critic, being much more interested in the girl. In a case like this, everyone is an initial suspect. An unguarded remark, or even just a look, could reveal volumes.

"Be my guest," Helvi said. "It isn't quite finished."

Mason eased himself from his comfortable seat and crossed to the window.

"Think I can see what you're getting at," he declared, after a few moments.

"No need to be polite," Helvi said. "My friends mostly do not like my work. Even I am not sure if I have talent."

"I'm no real judge," Mason said, candidly, "especially regarding abstract art. Never really got past the Impressionists."

Helvi laughed out loud. "In my country," she explained, "art has traditionally been limited to nationalist and folklore themes, to emphasize our identity as an independent country. Now we are trying to be more experimental."

Mason sensed that he might soon be drawn into a deeper discussion about art than he was capable of, and changed the subject.

"I once considered a career in architecture," he confessed. "But I became a policeman instead."

"That was a pity," she replied, with genuine feeling.

Mason shrugged. Few people got to lead a life of their own choosing. This girl was lucky. Her precise relationship to John Ormond was more important. He sipped the strong coffee while framing what could be interpreted as a rather delicate question.

"You wanted to know about John," she said, anticipating him.

"I suspect there is more to this than a simple case of disappearance. Scores of people vanish every year and nobody thinks all that much about it."

"You implied that he did not, in fact, return to England."

"Is that what you really thought?" he asked.

"Only as the most plausible explanation at the time. But as the weeks went by, with no word from him, I did not think that very likely."

"You were close friends?"

"We were good friends," she said neutrally, sinking back into the armchair cushions. There was a certain Nordic coolness in the way she spoke those words that might possibly be taken for indifference. Footsteps became audible from an adjoining room.

"Uncle Paavo," she explained, in answer to his unspoken question. "He owns this apartment."

"And you are a sub-tenant?"

She nodded. "At first I wanted my own place, but accommodation is scarce in Helsinki, and expensive."

His eye took in the details of the room. It was furnished in very good taste, with hand-woven rugs on the walls, wood sculptures of typical Finnish fauna and comfortable modern furniture. Uncle Paavo evidently did very well for himself.

"When was the last time you met him?" he asked.

Helvi knew at once, without thinking. "It would be April 28th, the day after my birthday. He took me to dinner at a restaurant in Kulosaari."

"Did you notice anything unusual about him? Did he seem depressed, for example; or worried?"

"I should say he was preoccupied. Less talkative than usual."

"Did he give a reason?"

"No. I assumed it was on account of his translation business. He'd been doing conference work in Turku the day before.

Originally we had planned to meet on my birthday, but he rang the night before to re-arrange. He explained that he couldn't get back to Helsinki in time for dinner because the conference was running late."

The telephone rang from the hallway. Helvi rose to answer it and Mason sat forward on the edge of the sofa to mull over this new information. Ormond's movements in that final week were beginning to fall into place. Turku, he knew, was a city on the south-west coast and the former capital of Finland when it had been under Swedish rule. His compatriot evidently moved around a lot. He again heard footsteps from the adjoining room, wondering why Uncle Paavo didn't come in and introduce himself.

"Did you and John meet often?" he enquired when she returned.

"We had an arrangement," she replied. "He came over here most Mondays when he was in town. We gave him dinner and he helped us improve our English. Uncle Paavo and me, that is."

Mason was disappointed at how prosaic that sounded, when he had thought there must be more to it than that from the way Helvi's name was heavily inked over in Ormond's diary.

"And that's how you became good friends?"

"We got to know each other well," she said, "because my uncle was sometimes away on business and John would come whether or not."

"Just the two of you? A friendly conversation over dinner."

Helvi flushed slightly and nodded.

"Did you know any of his other friends?" he asked, hoping that she could narrow them down to the most significant ones.

"I got the impression he didn't know a lot of people here," she said. "He was—how do you say in English—a lone wolf?"

"What makes you say that?" he asked, recalling a similar observation of Greenwood's.

"The way he talked about his life in England."

"You knew he didn't have much family?"

"He was orphaned as a boy. His only close relative was an aunt, living somewhere in the north."

"Did you feel a bit sorry for him?"

"Not sorry, exactly. But there was sympathy between us. I lost my parents in a skiing accident some years ago."

"Were you in love with him?" he asked, bluntly.

Helvi flushed again, but appeared unfazed by his question.

"When we first met," she said, evasively, "I was engaged to a Swedish university student named Sture. But he had to return to Sweden for family reasons. We eventually broke it off. I think he met someone else."

"I hope you don't think I am being too inquisitive," he said.

"Not at all," she replied. "It is your business to ask questions. Some more coffee?"

Mason declined. It would only keep him awake. But he did accept another slice of the delicious *pulla*.

"What sort of topics did you discuss at these private dinners?" he asked, hoping to get some insight into the workings of Ormond's mind.

"When my uncle was present, we discussed rather serious topics like art, music and literature. Left to ourselves, well, we just chatted."

"No politics?"

"Only in a very general way. What was going on in the news."

"Did he have a particular viewpoint?"

"I should say his views were rather left-wing, if anything. He used to have long discussions with Uncle Paavo about social services, health, trade unions and so on. Paavo took the opposite view, favoring privatization and free markets."

"That would not make him a socialist," Mason said. "Most English people would defend the the National Health Service and social security programs."

"With John I think it went deeper than that. He had in mind a different sort of social system altogether, one based more on cooperation than competition, catering to people's real needs rather than to commercial profit. I tended to side with him, against my uncle, who thought he was an idealist, someone not living in the real world."

Mason smiled, recalling similar notions of social justice he had entertained as a student. Yet the introduction of a possible political element threw an interesting new complexion on the case.

"You can always reach me at the Music Exchange," Helvi said, as he rose to take his leave. "If I can be of further help."

"Just one more thing," he said. "Does the name Maxim mean anything to you?"

She pondered for a moment, then shook her head. "I know no one of that name."

As he walked back across the park to his hotel, he mulled over the possible implications of Helvi's contribution, revisiting in his mind the impression he had briefly entertained at the Kulosaari apartment, that left-leaning Ormond had gone over to the other side. He might even, for all Mason knew, still be in Finland; gone underground with his Russian friend Maxim. Mannerheim was practically deserted by the time he reached it, save for patrons emerging from the Swedish Theater. The Three Counts was on the point of closing, which did not prevent him from glancing up at the mezzanine windows on the off-chance the bearded gentleman had returned. There was, however, no sign of him. He hurried the last hundred yards to the Marski and headed straight to the bar for a night-cap. A double-Scotch was in order, to help him thaw.

CHAPTER FOUR

THE SAUNA AT Hotel Kivi opened its doors to the general public at noon, reserving the morning hours for hotel guests. Since it was a regular haunt of the missing translator, and since he himself had never before experienced the Finnish bath, George Mason decided to pay it a visit following his morning conference with Major Forsenius and a light lunch at the station buffet. He located the establishment, situated in a narrow side-street, easily enough with the aid of his city plan, paid the fee of 50 Finnmarks and tentatively entered. The sauna attendant, at once marking him as a novice, showed him personally to the changing-room with a flood of advice in Finnish that the detective only vaguely understood. Left to his own devices, he disrobed and placed his belongings neatly in the small locker, slipping the rubber band holding the key over his left wrist. He had already quit the changing-room when he noticed he was still wearing his wristwatch. Unsure if it was waterproof, he returned to put it in the locker, casting a critical eye on his waistline as he did so. Whatever else transpired, the sauna would be sure to do him good.

Feeling a bit unsure of himself, he pushed open the heavy door leading to the main area of the sauna. It was a few moments before his eyes accustomed themselves to the unfamiliar surroundings, to the wall of steam and heat coming towards him. At intervals on the tiled floor were simple wooden stools occupied by naked men who were being alternately scrubbed with soap or doused with pails of cold water by sturdy women in white aprons and rubber boots. They did not flinch or cry out at this Spartan treatment, but sat gazing impassively before them in a posture of endurance. One of the *saunatajat* motioned Mason towards a second door on the right. He picked his way gingerly across tiles swimming in soapy water, taking care not to slip and impressed by the total silence of the place. Not one word was uttered.

As he opened the second door a rush of hot air greeted him. He closed it quickly behind him, perceiving dim figures sitting or lying flat on wooden benches that rose up in three separate tiers above the stove. Their bodies glistened with sweat. Mason groped his way forward and, as he did so, a helpful bather rose at once from his place, grasped a small wooden board, doused it briefly under the cold water tap and gave it to him to sit on. The detective took the hint, feeling the heat of the bench with his bare palm, glad that he hadn't placed his haunches firmly upon it. A novice could do himself an injury in a place like this. Taking his place, he remembered to observe Forsenius's advice not to stay too long on his first-ever visit. A glance at the thermometer showed a reading of 120 degrees Celsius. He thanked the helpful individual, who smiled and then retreated behind the wall of silence which filled the small chamber. None of the other bathers seemed to have noticed him, so intent were they on sweating it out and enduring the extreme heat.

They might almost have been asleep, so still and impassive were they. Finns were like that, he reflected: calm as a deep lake, brooding as the pine-forest that covered vast areas of the country. Unlikely allies in a police enquiry. Yet John Ormond came here at this hour almost every week. Someone must have seen him and possibly spoken with him, if they spoke at all.

Sensing his body heat rising quickly and uncomfortably, and doubting his powers of endurance for more than fifteen minutes, he would have to work quickly if his visit to the Kivi sauna was to become anything more than an interesting slimming exercise. In the wash-room it was all scrub and splash; no chance to speak to anyone. In the hot-room, conversation seemed taboo.

He watched in silent fascination as beads of sweat formed at every pore, joined forces with each other and formed little rivulets down his skin. He felt his limbs yielding to the therapy and a deep relaxation setting in. The last thing he needed was to fall asleep. He thought of Japan, another country with a highly-developed bath-culture, where the female attendants would be much younger. Here they were like laundresses, regarding their male charges as so much soiled linen. He left the chamber, took a cold shower and came back. The door opened and closed, as bathers left in pools of sweat and others came in. He contemplated his limbs, normally pale and rather flabby, turning bright pink. The atmosphere became increasingly close; breath came in shorter spasms; yet he was determined to stick it out, to get his money's worth.

The chamber suddenly cleared, save for himself and the helpful Finn lying full-length on the tier just above him. Growing aware again of his surroundings, he raised himself on one elbow, recognized his companion and smiled encouragingly.

"You all right?" he asked.

Mason turned slowly towards him. In the sauna all movements were slow. Through the heat-haze he looked into the man's guileless blue eyes, considered him trustworthy.

"Do you always keep the temperature so high?" he said.

"It's about average," the Finn replied. "But you must take care not to overdo it. I see you are not accustomed to the Finnish bath."

Mason felt piqued that it was so obvious. The Finn sat up, fully alert again and prepared to take a keener interest in this intriguing visitor.

"Here on business?" he enquired.

"In a manner of speaking, yes."

"Timber? Textiles?"

"Personal business," Mason replied. "As a matter of fact, I was hoping to meet an old acquaintance of mine, who used this hour."

"Perhaps he has not yet arrived."

"Or I have the wrong sauna."

"English, like yourself?" the Finn asked, doubtfully. "I come here at least twice a month, over many years. But I have met few English. Swedes and Danes, yes; the odd German."

Mason was beginning to feel he had had enough heat. He wiped the sweat from his face, rose slowly and turned to the door. Through the small window he observed the scrubbings and the dowsings going on in the adjoining room, as the brisk *saunatajat* went about their business.

"Wait a minute," the Finn said. "There was an English who spoke Finnish very well, whom I met earlier this year. Haven't seen him for many months."

"Who lived in Kulosaari?" Mason asked at once.

"He may well have done."

"Do you know what he did here, for a living?"

"He was a translator of some sort, I believe. Worked at the Polyglot Institute. I remember well because I once took English lessons there myself, some years ago."

"Have you any idea where I might find him?" Mason asked, confident that they were talking about Ormond.

"Try the Institute," the other said. "It's on Mikonkatu, near the main station."

"Already have. They've lost contact with him."

"Try the police station then. They keep tabs on all foreign residents by renewing resident permits annually."

"I was hoping to keep the local police out of it," Mason replied, evasively. "My friend may be in some slight personal difficulty."

The Finn scratched his head, looking both philosophical and sympathetic at the same time.

"You might try the Havis Club on Annankatu," he finally suggested. "I have seen him there, the odd occasion. Again, not since many months."

"Annankatu?"

"Down by Hotel Clovis, just off Mannerheim."

"What kind of club might that be?" Mason enquired, recalling that Ormond had also been a member of the Marlowe.

"A restaurant and a nightclub combined."

"With girls, cabaret, the usual things?"

The helpful Finn nodded, with a knowing smile.

"It has a certain reputation," he added. "The sort of place where we like to take visiting businessmen for a little relaxation after working hours. After sauna, of course."

"Do you go there yourself?"

"From time to time. I am in the timber industry. We have a lot of foreign clients to entertain."

"The translator. When you saw him, was he with other people? With business contacts perhaps?"

"No. He was always alone, sitting at the bar drinking campari. Sometimes he stayed for the floor show, but generally left quite early."

Mason thanked the Finn and quit the hot chamber for the adjoining wash-room. Beneath the shower, as his body temperature plunged rapidly to more normal levels, he went over in his mind the odd pieces of information he had gleaned. The Polyglot Institute, the Kilpinens, Maxim and now the Havis Club. There was as yet no obvious connection between them. This case was becoming more complex and interesting every day, with some unexpected perks like his maiden visit to a sauna. Glancing an apprehensive eye at one of the vacant stools, he prepared to submit himself manfully to the services of a waiting *saunataja* ominously brandishing scrubbing-brush and carbolic soap. Following this dire treatment and the customary rest period on one of the beds in the third and final chamber of the sauna suite, there would just be sufficient time to visit some of the city bookshops before they closed for the day.

Feeling several pounds lighter and fresh as a mountain spring, the enterprising detective tried a few bookshops in the city center before entering the premises of Academic Bookshop on Mannerheim which, he had been told at his last call, was the main importer of foreign books. Since all imported reading material was purchased through a central government agency, the obliging assistant was able to tell him what he needed to know about the Russian-language edition of Mikhail Sholokov's epic novel, *Quiet Flows the Don* signed by Maxim, that he had discovered at the Kulosaari apartment. That it was far from being an unusual acquisition, Mason realized the moment he was shown the store's large display of foreign literature, in which books of Russian origin were quite well represented.

All the assistant could tell him with certainty was that Ormond's copy did in fact bear the sales code of Academic Bookshop. Checking her computer records, she discovered that it had been purchased late in April, not many days before it had been given to the translator, and had been part of a spring consignment of Russian books, most of which had now been sold. Since the novel itself was nothing out of the ordinary, his interest focused mainly on the donor; but it seemed hardly likely that the young sales assistant would remember that far back who had bought a copy of a well-known novel. Helvi knew nothing of Maxim, either, reinforcing what Greenwood told him, that Ormond's social life was compartmentalized. The police would have records on all foreign residents, assuming they were here legitimately and had registered with the authorities for annual residence permits. He crossed to the English section and scanned the paperbacks, mainly out of curiosity about which British authors were popular here, rather than from any desire for reading material. He had enough to occupy his mind.

Returning eventually to the Marski, he stretched out on his bed and fell fast asleep. Fighting against it all the way from

Hotel Kivi, the effect of the sauna finally caught up with him, his last waking thought being that a man his age should be more careful of extreme exertion. Sauna was something to accustom oneself to gradually. His conversation with the helpful timber expert had prolonged his stay in the hot-room. Without realizing it, he had overdone things.

He was roused one hour later by the incessant ringing of his bedside telephone. He sat up with a start, picked up the receiver and glanced at his watch. It was nearly six.

"A Major Forsenius is here to see you," said the reception clerk.

"Send him up at once," Mason replied, hoping that his drowsiness hadn't inconvenienced the Finn.

"Been trying to reach you all afternoon," Forsenius announced the moment he entered, casting a faintly critical eye on the rather disheveled state of his English counterpart. "So I decided to come here in person, in case something had happened. Been in a fight?"

"Nothing more strenuous than the Finnish sauna," Mason retorted, ruefully.

Forsenius chuckled, evidently as amused as he was intrigued.

"Got the case sewn up already, have you? Decided to take the afternoon off."

Mason simply scowled; but the nap had certainly refreshed him. He was amazed at how much lighter and fitter he felt after just one visit.

"Just following leads," he explained. "Seems John Ormond was a regular patron of the Kivi sauna."

"And you were expecting to find him there?"

"Hardly that, Major. But it proved its worth. I discovered another of Ormond's favorite haunts, the Havis Club on Annankatu."

"Watch your step if you go there," Forsenius said, jocularly. "We raid it regularly, once a month."

"Is the joint that bad?" asked Mason, in some surprise.

"In connection with our strict laws on the sale of alcohol," Forsenius explained. "It has a history of illegal imports of liquor, mainly vodka and whisky."

"Is that your only problem? A bit of boot-legging?"

"All alcohol for re-sale must be purchased through the State monopoly. Infringements lead to heavy fines and possible withdrawal of licenses. We haven't closed the Havis down because it's one of the few places to entertain foreign visitors."

"Don't you think that, with such strict licensing laws, you will only cause more problems in the long run? Look what happened in America under Prohibition."

"We choose to do things in our own way," the major said, curtly. "What suits one society may not always work elsewhere. Which brings me to the main point of my visit. There is some result from your enquiry about Paavo Kilpinen, related in fact to what we were just discussing."

"You mean Paavo's a boot-legger?" said Mason, in disbelief.

"Perhaps we should take a short drive around town," Forsenius said. "Hotel rooms are not the securest of places. My car is waiting behind the hotel."

The detective smoothed his hair in the stand mirror and slipped on his coat and hat. The Finn led the way downstairs and round to the back of the premises to the unmarked car, a black Chaika of Russian make. The rear door opened as if by invisible hand and as they sank back into the deep upholstery the powerful engine revved and the car sped forward along Mannerheim, coming to an abrupt halt ten minutes later at the crest of a steep drive overlooking both South Harbor and the Brunnspark, the former ringed with lights, the latter in near-total darkness.

"Aren't we somewhere near the Kilpinens' place now?" Mason asked.

"Their apartment just is down there, to the left. We call this the diplomatic quarter, since most of the foreign embassies are located here."

"So what have you turned up about Uncle Paavo?"

"He had a brush with the law two years ago, for vodka-running along the coastal route from the border town of Vyborg."

"In contravention of Finnish law?"

"For many years now," Forsenius explained, "we have operated a strict licensing policy. Restaurants and bars are, of course, exempt; but no individual citizen may purchase liquor without presenting an alcohol permit. These are issued automatically to every Finn once he attains his majority."

"How on earth do you get away with it?' Mason wanted to know.

"Finns in general are very law-abiding people, but there are always exceptions. Some people smuggle liquor; others distill their own in the forests, a type of wood brandy called *jaloviina.*"

"And Paavo was one of the smugglers?"

"In a minor way, admittedly; but quite successfully over a period of years."

"Would that account for his apparent affluence? For his beautiful apartment in this exclusive area?"

"I doubt he made much money from it. More for private consumption, I gather; rather than as a commercial venture."

"I would hardly consider him a criminal on that score."

"He wasn't in fact convicted of anything, just given a heavy caution on account of his standing in the business community. He runs a profitable antique-dealership."

Mason pondered this information for a few moments, while observing a lone skier crossing the snow-covered park in the darkness.

"Someone from the embassies," the major explained, noting his interest. "You can see them at almost any hour of the day. When the sea freezes over, you'll see them there as well."

"What you say about Uncle Paavo may be of interest," Mason said, pushing thoughts of the Dolomites from his mind, "if he knew of safe routes along the southern coast towards

Leningrad, avoiding check-points. Smuggling people rather than vodka, however, would be more to the point."

"I get your drift," Forsenius said sardonically, as the Chaika's engine started up and nosed slowly down towards Mannerheim. "But that's a pretty long pitch. How would Ormond tie in with Kilpinen?"

"Through his niece, Helvi."

"Go on."

"Ormond made regular weekly visits to their apartment, to give them both conversation practise. The niece works at the Music Exchange. Her number was in the pocket-diary handed to you by the *talomies*."

"You've already checked her out?"

"Last evening, in fact. I should say she is completely above board, in so far as anyone can be in this puzzling state of affairs. Don't suppose she was involved in the vodka-running?"

"We have nothing on a Helvi Kilpinen."

"So she may not even know of her uncle's caution?"

Forsenius shrugged. "He may, or may not, have mentioned it to her."

"Helvi's an art student part-time, at the Academy. She struck me as very genuine and dedicated to the arts in general."

"We are an artistic people," Forsenius said, with pride. "Finnish design, in textiles, glassware, pottery is world-famous."

"How about authors?" Mason asked.

"Our most famous author is Alexis Kivi. His play *The Cobblers on the Heath* is performed every Christmas. You should look out for it."

"Do you know any Russian authors?"

The major gave him an odd look, as if wondering what sort of question that was.

"Everyone knows Tolstoy, Dostoyevsky, Pushkin and so on. The list is endless."

"About the time John Ormond disappeared," Mason said, as the Chaika drew up in front of his hotel. "a leading contemporary Russian writer named Timor Tarkov turned up in the West. Probably right here, on your own doorstep, in transit to Switzerland, where he now resides."

"You know about Tarkov? "the Finn asked, in considerable surprise.

"His picture was in your newspapers very recently. You could see it in any bar."

Forsenius fell silent, pondering matters. Somewhere behind them, a ship's siren pierced the night.

"The night ferry to Stockholm," he explained.

"More smuggling?" quipped Mason.

"The wrong route," replied the other.

"Care to join me over a drink?" Mason asked, expectantly.

"It's against the rules while on duty," the Finn replied. "You order your *jaloviina*. I'll make do with coffee." He gave instructions to his driver, then stepped out of the car with the detective. A few moments later, they were comfortably ensconced in the armchairs of the Marski bar, which was relatively quiet in the hour before dinner.

"Correct me if I'm wrong," Forsenius said. "But do I detect a certain line of reasoning in your fertile mind?" He paused for a moment and sipped his coffee. "You are perhaps thinking there may be some connection between Ormond's disappearance and Tarkov's defection, Paavo Kilpinen being somehow the link-man."

"Not bad tipple," Mason said, referring to the wood brandy. "Palatable; but I'd rather have a single malt any day."

"Well?" prompted the other.

"Something along those lines."

"An ingenious hypothesis, certainly."

"Let us suppose there was sufficient resemblance between the two—Tarkov and Ormond, I mean—for a switch to be made at, say, some obscure border crossing."

"You are suggesting that it was Kilpinen and Ormond who entered Russia; whereas it was Kilpinen and Tarkov who came out."

"As a working hypothesis."

"Then you have to account for Ormond. Where would he be now, languishing in some Russian prison on a trumped-up charge of, let us say, economic espionage?"

"Couldn't he equally have 'disappeared' when he had served his purpose? The border between Finland and Russia is a wild and desolate area, extending hundreds of miles."

"In that case you will never find him," Forsenius said, helping himself to a slice of *pulla*. "If we could establish that Kilpinen and Ormond entered Russia together . . ."

"That shouldn't be too difficult," Mason said. "Wouldn't they both have needed visas from the Russian Embassy here in Helsinki?"

"As a rule, the embassy is very secretive. You couldn't rely on them for accurate information. Disinformation is more their territory."

"Then we must do our own checking up," Mason said, emphatically.

"I'll do what I can for you, discreetly," Forsenius promised. "We cannot officially re-open the case."

"Helvi has been sharing her uncle's apartment for quite some time now. She ought to know something of his recent movements. I gather he goes abroad quite a lot, probably in connection with his antiques business."

"Anything else occur to you?"

"There's also an individual going by the name of Maxim, who presented Ormond with a Russian novel sometime in April. I wonder if you could check if he had a valid residence permit?"

"That's all you have to go off, his first name?" Forsenius said. "Don't forget that hundreds of White Russians moved here during the Revolution. Many of their male descendants could be called Maxim. It's a fairly common name."

"I suspect this Maxim wears a beard, in a country of clean-shaven men." He instinctively stroked his own chin, feeling the two days' growth of stubble.

"That should narrow the field down," the Finn agreed. "We keep photographs of all residence applicants. I'll have someone in back-up look into it for you as soon as possible."

"I'll call you in a couple of days," Mason said.

Forsenius drained his coffee and left the bar, leaving the detective with an hour to pass before dinner. Feeling invigorated by the sauna, he decided to take a walk through the wintry city, mainly to watch the departure of the night ferry to Stockholm, whose siren on arrival at South Harbor they had heard from their parked car, indulging an interest in shipping of all types dating from his days on regular beat in London's dockland, and also to check the layout of the small port in case it should prove useful in his enquiries. He proceeded along Mannerheim, turned left into Esplanade and soon reached the market square. The vendors who arrived by boat most mornings had long-since departed and the whole area was invested with a profound silence. Residential tenements filled out the silvery skyline, with lights visible from the inhabited islands of the archipelago. Helsinki was home to not more than half a million souls, making it one of the smaller European capitals; yet it had all the amenities of a major city. Its size made for optimum convenience getting about and there was the added advantage, from a professional point of view, that crime was kept to a minimum. Or so the major maintained.

A statue-group with fountains played softly in the evening light as he strolled past the deserted harbor towards the Customs House on one of the outer quays where ocean-going liners berthed. He was just in time to watch the majestic ship inch away from the shore and head slowly out towards the center of the bay, skirting the large island housing the yacht club before turning south-west towards Stockholm. He made out the name *Allotar* on the stern, following its slow progress until the lights on the port side faded into the night. Soon after its departure, the Customs House and adjacent amenities closed down for the night. What a large extent of waterfront to lie for many hours in darkness, he reflected, as he turned back towards the city. It could provide cover for almost any illicit trade, with small craft slipping in unobserved, importing vodka, whisky or whatever else seemed profitable and worth the risk to sidestep the licensing policies of the Finnish capital. People too could appear as from nowhere, and as easily disappear. It seemed as likely a place as any as the site of John Ormond's sudden exodus.

CHAPTER FIVE

G EORGE MASON DID not anticipate having to argue his way into the Havis Club, but the athletic-looking bouncer was adamant that visitors must wear a tie. He was loathe to retrace his steps to the hotel in the cold and decided to try and face it out. If persuasion failed, he could always use his rank, something he was reluctant to do. It was better for his purposes to appear much like an ordinary tourist than a detective on a missing person mission. The bouncer was verbally tackling a half-lit Finn also seeking entry. As the door was about to close in both their faces, Mason produced his British passport. This did the trick. The detective was allowed in, the Finn shut out, underlining the strictness of the alcohol laws even at a venue implicated in devious vodka dealings.

A narrow flight of stairs led up to a large, dimly-lit restaurant already full to overflowing. He groped his way to the bar and ordered a brandy, while his eye reconnoitered the place. It was a night-club much like any other he had visited, whether in an official or unofficial capacity, except that the trio of musicians were all female, performing jazzed-up Bach on a small dais by the dance-floor, just now being prepared for the cabaret. The atmosphere was subdued, in anticipation of the imminent start of the show. Mason sipped his drink and listened appreciatively to the trio, broadening his perception of the great composer.

It was some minutes before he realized that the Havis clientele consisted very largely of people older than he was. The males were seated together on one side of the dance-floor, the females on the other. Communication between them was frequent and conducted by means of a house telephone system. Above each table was a large illuminated cube with that table's number clearly visible. The women from time to time picked up their receivers and listened, to what Mason imagined were either sweet nothings or requests for a dance following the cabaret. Occasionally the women took the initiative. If he sat down, he thought, he might get fixed up for the evening. It was all very formal and polite and that appealed to his old-fashioned values. At the same time, he could not help wondering what attractions such an environment had for a young man like John Ormond. Search as he did, he could not discern through the gloom a face approximating in age to the missing translator's.

Had Ormond come here for some specific purpose, other than to socialize? The helpful Finn at the Kivi sauna claimed to have seen him here several times, but always apparently at the bar where Mason was now standing, alone and drinking campari. He decided to sound out the barman, who was nearby polishing glasses.

"Trying to trace a friend of mine," he said. "He used to come here regularly." He gave the man a description close to that provided by Forsenius, via the *talomies.*

The barman pondered for a moment, but looked doubtful. "How recently?" he asked.

"About six months ago."

"Can't help you then. I have been working here only since midsummer. I have a Swedish friend who might fit that description, but he went to America last month. Besides, this was not his type of club."

"I imagine not," the detective said. "But thanks anyway."

The manager then made a brief announcement in both Finnish and English, quickly followed onto the floor by a svelte young woman dressed entirely in black. The trio abruptly changed mood and tempo, Bach being set aside for a popular tune he vaguely recognized. The lights were dimmed even further, to almost total darkness, as the men at the bar moved closer to watch the performance of Lulu, from Rumania. Mason was intrigued at the extent of Finland's ties with the East European countries. They traded in timber, textiles, machinery and ice-breakers, apparently even in exotic dancers. His restless mind was already at work as she went through the preliminary motions of her routine. She would be an ideal courier, in one city this week, another the next, crossing easily from east to west. As her lissome form swayed to the rhythms of the music, she was an *agent provocateuse* in a different sense. The mature women also looked on with interest, as if reminded of their youth. Her dark eyes were expressionless, Mason thought; fixed on some distant star. There was scant rapport between artiste and audience, of the type most performers cherish. All a bit too matter-of-fact, right up until the final flourish when the room was plunged in total darkness, as her naked figure disappeared into the wings, to an enthusiastic handclap from both the men and the women.

He bought a beer and moved with it to the men's tables, several of which were now vacant, their former occupants having transferred with the aid of phone calls to the women's section. Segregation, it seemed, was only for the start of the game; perhaps even a gimmick to heighten interest in the opposite sex. He watched the budding romances with an amused detachment, thought of Adele and their planned skiing vacation, wondering if it would ever materialize. The phone on his table suddenly rang, catching him off-guard.

"Good evening, Mr Mason," said a thickly-accented voice on the other end of the line. "I hope that you enjoyed the show."

He felt a sudden panic and a tight sensation in the pit of his stomach. It had been foolish of him to sit in such an obvious position; he must be visible from almost every part of the room. His eyes searched the now dimly-lit room warily, to penetrate the smoke-haze on the far side of the dance-floor, his senses alert to danger.

"Who is this?" he asked, half hoping it was some practical joke on the part of Forsenius, or even of Greenwood.

"You are wasting your time, Mr Mason. You will not find what you are looking for."

"But who is this speaking?" he blurted angrily, realizing that, in the hiatus following Lulu's exit, his voice carried across the room, earning mute looks of disapproval from those nearest to him. With an ominous click, the line went dead.

Quite stunned, and with the uneasy sensation that it was he who had been stripped naked, he quickly downed his drink and made for the exit. The crisp night air cleared his head of the fuggy atmosphere of the club. At least, he reflected, he had struck a responsive chord: there *was* more than a casual connection between the missing translator and the Havis Club. But how did the mysterious caller know his name, something only the police and the hotel clerk knew?

*

He awoke late again the following morning, putting it down to the lingering effects of the sauna and the drinks he had consumed at the Havis Club. The cathedral clock struck nine as he eased his frame off the spartan mattress—the Finns for some reason preferred hard beds—considering it one of the few perks of his present assignment that he was not governed by the clock. Completing his toilet unhurriedly, he dressed and made his way to The Three Counts for a late breakfast and to plan his campaign for the day ahead. The surprise phone call to his table came to mind as he collected porridge and egg-with-anchovy sandwiches—the nearest approximation to an English breakfast—and took it to the window seat he was beginning to regard as his own. Overnight there had been more snow and the snowplows were at work along Mannerheim. The trams were snaking slowly up and down, building to a queue where the line forked at Esplanade, to run down to the harbor or forge straight ahead to the Brunnspark. Their normally well-oiled, muted progress had given way to the grinding sound of metal against bare metal, in a kind of morning raga music to the stirring city, punctuated by the occasional blast of an impatient motorist's horn.

The restaurant was pleasantly warm and deserted save for a table of young people he identified as office staff holding a morning briefing over coffee. Beyond the picture windows, the denizens of Helsinki went briskly about their business. Harsh winters were something they had adapted to long ago in the history of the race and heavy snow caused only minimal disruption to their routine. Even the sea-lanes across the Baltic remained open year-round, by the powerful ice-breakers they were so skilled at building and which formed one of Finland's main exports. He did, however, sympathize with the policeman on point duty by the Swedish Theater. God knows how long he had been there in his fur hat, ear-muffs and ankle-length greatcoat, flapping his arms across his chest to maintain circulation.

His light meal was satisfying and the porridge—*puuro*, on the menu—warmed him nicely after his short walk from the hotel. Returning to the counter for a re-fill of coffee, he revised the details of the case so far. There was Helvi Kilpinen, who had been Ormond's close friend, if not girl-friend; Greenwood, the rather devious proprietor of the Polyglot Institute; Uncle Paavo, the antiques dealer with the improbable record of vodka smuggling; a defecting Russian academician and a second Russian entity, the mysterious Maxim. Added to all these interesting individuals was the unknown caller over the love-lines of the Havis Club. Evidently, Mason's presence in Helsinki was now obvious to the opposition, whoever they may be. They were predicting failure. But what precisely did they mean by that? Failure to locate John Ormond or to discover the sensitive material presumed to be in his possession? On the other hand, the call could have been just a bluff, designed to throw him off the scent.

It was time, he considered, for another meeting with Helvi, in the hope that she could throw some light on her uncle's movements during the spring. Why not ring the Music Exchange and invite her over here for a spot of lunch? It was conveniently close and he could spend the intervening time, just under two hours, paying a second visit to the Polyglot Institute. He drained his cup and briefly scanned the headlines of the morning papers before quitting the restaurant and heading for the rank of telephone booths outside the theater. She will be surprised, he thought, to hear from me again so soon.

"Helsingin Musikki," came a dulcet female voice over the line.

"May I speak with Helvi Kilpinen?" he enquired.

He heard the clatter of the receiver on the wooden counter and, in the background, the strains of a Mozart symphony, which he began to finger-tap on the telephone book. The *Linz*, he soon decided.

"Kilpinen," came an equally melodious voice. He pictured the pale oval face behind it, fringed with ash-blond hair.

"George Mason here," he said, breezily. "We met two days ago, remember?"

"Of course I remember you," she replied, her voice betraying surprise.

"I need to talk with you again," he explained. "But not over the telephone."

"I'm sure I already told you everything I know about John," she said, guardedly. "But if you're sure it will help . . ."

"Thought we might meet for lunch. If you're free, that is."

She seemed hesitant. In the background, Mozart had suddenly given way to Delius. Customers were evidently testing Christmas purchases. He had to jam the receiver to his ear to catch her reply.

"That's kind of you, Mr Mason. But I have only one hour free and I have shopping to do."

"I could do it for you," he quickly offered, "beforehand."

"You couldn't possibly," she laughed. "It's for a birthday present, for my uncle."

"Couldn't you do it later, say after work?"

"The stores close at four," she said. "But I could just as well buy it tomorrow. No particular hurry."

"Twelve o'clock then?"

"But where? Perhaps you don't know our restaurants very well."

"Gastronomic Helsinki, no." he admitted. "How about The Three Counts across from the Swedish Theater? It's a self-service, but the food is quite good."

"I know the place. I went there a few times with John. Let's make it 12.15."

"12.15 it shall be," the detective said, ringing off.

He left the booth with a feeling of relief. She might just as well have refused his invitation. That she accepted reinforced his impression that she herself was probably above suspicion and may not even have known of her uncle's past record. As he trudged through the fresh snow towards Mikonkatu, the prospect of entertaining the attractive Helvi to lunch cheered him and fortified him against the hostile elements. It was with a lighter step that he covered the half-mile or so to the Polyglot Institute.

The establishment was a hive of activity as groups of Finns, whose pallid cheeks alone had been exposed to the wintry air, were arriving for mid-morning sessions carrying English textbooks. It was the modern trend for them to learn his language; a generation ago they would have been equally dedicated students of German, to provide vital links with the wider world.

The secretary, Mrs Virtanen, showed him into Greenwood's private office. While awaiting the proprietor's appearance from the classrooms, Mason made a quick inspection of the room, hoping to light upon some detail that may have eluded him on his first visit. He found nothing. The Polyglot seemed above reproach, just another academic institution with its own rarified atmosphere, an outpost of British culture with a union jack and the Finnish flag side by side on the cluttered desk. As Arthur Greenwood confronted him again in the open doorway, there was a perceptible narrowing of the man's eyes that did not escape the detective.

"What can we do for you today, Inspector?" Greenwood asked curtly, without offering his hand. "I already told you all I know about John Ormond."

"My apologies, Mr Greenwood," Mason said, insincerely, "if I'm taking up your valuable time. Investigations like this take a while and we have to be very thorough, leave no stone unturned."

"Of course, of course," flustered Greenwood. "Perhaps it would be better if you made an appointment in advance. I've just had to dismiss a class early on your account."

Mason took the point, averting his gaze from the prickly proprietor to the calendar on the wall behind his desk. It was an English calendar, showing a picture of the harbor at Mevagissy that reminded him wistfully of home.

"Well?" asked Greenwood. "What's new?"

"It appears," replied Mason, clearing his throat, "that Ormond has simply vanished. We have no leads whatsoever."

"So much I understood from Major Forsenius, months ago," the other said, testily.

"Doesn't it strike you as rather odd that an employee of this institute should disappear, entirely without trace?"

Greenwood shrugged.

"The point I'm trying to make," Mason persisted, "is whether or not there is some connection between his work as a translator and his disappearance."

The proprietor looked non-plussed. "How do you mean?" he asked.

"I need to know more about the exact nature of his work." He sensed that Greenwood felt ill at ease, that his gruffness was merely subterfuge.

"Ormond was engaged mainly on commercial and legal texts, trade agreements, export documents, labor contracts and suchlike."

"From Finnish into English?"

"No. Our Mrs Virtanen handles that. She's perfectly bilingual. Her mother was Scottish, her father Finnish. Ormond worked mainly from Swedish, Finland's second official language, and occasionally from Russian."

"Into Finnish or English?"

"English. Our translators always work into their mother tongue."

Mason pondered for a moment. "The Russian work, where did that originate?"

"Always from the same source, the Russian Trade Commission."

"Did he go there to collect it?"

"It was delivered by courier from their embassy and picked up from here when completed."

"Is there a lot of trade between England and Russia?"

"Developing," Greenwood said, more amicably. "There's often a spate of translation activity when a new trade agreement has been signed. Then it tends to tail off. A pity, really; it's a lucrative field."

"Was Ormond your only expert in this field?"

"Correct. But it can be done—is now in fact being done in his absence—in a roundabout way, from Russian into Finnish, then from Finnish into English."

"Did Ormond have personal contacts with any of the Russian Embassy personnel?" Mason asked, hoping to identify a link.

"As I already explained, everything went through this office."

They were interrupted by a short rap on the glass panel of the office door. It opened to reveal Mrs Virtanen bearing a tray of coffee and *pulla*, which she placed on the desk in front of Greenwood.

"This is George Mason, all the way from London," Greenwood explained. "Inspector—Mrs Virtanen, my secretary."

The detective rose to shake her hand.

"We already met, briefly," she said. "How do you enjoy the Finnish winter?"

"Bearing up," he replied. "Your city streets would make good cross-country skiing terrain."

The secretary laughed and withdrew.

"Care to join me?" the proprietor asked, invitingly.

Mason accepted, keen to prolong the interview. "Does the name Timor Tarkov mean anything to you?" he asked as the refreshment was served.

"Seems to ring a bell."

"He's a Russian author, or so I understand," Mason said. "Can't claim to have read him, however."

Greenwood sipped his coffee thoughtfully. "Wait a minute," he said, eventually. "Isn't he the chap who surfaced here in Helsinki some months ago? I recall reading about it in the newspapers. *Helsingin Sanomat* did a big spread on him."

"Six months ago, almost to the day," Mason said.

"Is there some significance in that?" the proprietor asked, dubiously.

"There may be."

Greenwood smiled back at him, as if he had caught him in some schoolboy prank.

"What you are really asking me, Inspector, is if I know of any connection between Ormond and Tarkov."

"I'm going off Ormond's knowledge of Russian and the interesting coincidence of dates."

"Interesting, I would agree; but I must admit it had not occurred to me before today."

"You are not aware of any meeting between them?"

"Absolutely not. Yet it's ironic in a way. Ormond was very keen on getting literary translations. He thought his talents unfulfilled on routine commercial work. In fact, he used to sound out Mrs Virtanen on some types of work she did, travel articles, brochures, even some short fiction from time to time."

Greenwood then began to tap his fingers on the blotter, as if to signal that the interview should end. But Mason had one further question.

"Did Ormond show much interest in politics?" he asked.

"None whatsoever. But I was only his employer. I would not have expected him to discuss politics with me. I'm surprised you asked such a question."

Mason ignored the look of mild reproach, the irritating tone of moral superiority adopted by Greenwood.

"Did he ever, while he worked here, pass any remark that might be construed as either pro- or anti-Russian?"

"I should say he was Russophile, if anything. But that his interests were confined purely to artistic matters. To my knowledge he never once visited the country, despite its proximity."

"You mean he admired Russia for its cultural achievements, for its music, ballet, literature and so on?"

Greenwood nodded in agreement. "That was the impression I got. But then, as I said, he only worked here."

Mason thought of the contents of Ormond's bookshelves, and of his friendship with art-student Helvi. What the proprietor was saying fitted the picture he was building in his mind of his missing compatriot, but he felt sure there must be more to it than a genuine appreciation of Russian culture.

"If you will excuse me, Inspector," Greenwood said, rising from his chair. "I have a class starting in two minutes. Mrs Virtanen will show you out."

"I'll be in touch," the detective said. "Thanks for the coffee."

*

Helvi was waiting for him in the foyer as he walked in stamping the packed snow off his boots. He mumbled apologetically about the difficulties of navigating the snowbound streets. She merely chuckled, taking a particularly Finnish delight in the privations of foreigners. It was their own fault if they came in winter. The restaurant was already quite full, drawing its clientele from the suites of offices in the floors above and from the nearby IBM headquarters, an elegant structure in concrete and glass which did nothing to diminish the distinguished skyline of a city indebted to world-renowned architects Alvar Aalto and Eero Saarinen. Mason would have suggested a quieter establishment had he known of one and counted himself lucky that they found a spare table over in the corner. Having unloaded the contents of their trays, Helvi placed the book she was carrying face upwards on the table, distracting her companion from his food.

"Is something the matter?" she asked, eventually.

Mason looked directly into her candid blue eyes, at the rogue strand of blond hair he would gladly have leaned over and set perfectly in place.

"An interesting title you have there," he remarked.

"Timor Tarkov's *Echoes of the Steppes*. It's from my uncle's library. I borrowed it this morning to read in the tram."

"One of your uncle's books?"

"You do seem surprised," she said, between forkfuls of food.

"Just the coincidence," Mason said. "There was a piece about that author in the newspaper a couple of days ago."

"He defected to the West earlier this year. Have you read him?"

"Afraid not. My job leaves little time for reading."

"I'm enjoying it so far," Helvi said. "It's a very good translation, signed by the author."

"Does your uncle have other books by him? Is he an admirer?" Mason would be more than happy to establish a firm connection between Paavo Kilpinen and Timor Tarkov.

"An admirer, certainly; but only on the strength of this one book. It's the only one, so far as I know, to have been translated into Finnish."

"He has written other books?"

"At least two, prior to this. They date from his childhood and youth in the Urals. So Uncle Paavo tells me."

"Is your uncle an authority on Tarkov?"

"Hardly that. He doesn't read Russian."

"Really?" he replied, pushing his plate aside with only a vague impression that the light lunch had been good. He offered coffee and rose to fetch it from the self-service counter, feeling a bit more confident now of linking Uncle Paavo with Tarkov's defection, a scenario he had broached to the skeptical major.

"Your uncle is in antiques, I believe?"

"Paavo has many interests," she replied, unaware of any double meaning in her remark. "Since spring, for example, he has been giving a series of lectures at the Academy."

"On what topic?"

"Early Russian icons."

"Not my field at all," Mason quipped, with a gesture of feigned despair.

She smiled her faintly enigmatic smile, he thought in condescension to his ignorance of such matters.

"Do these varied interests take him abroad from time to time?"

"Occasionally," she replied. "Mainly to the Scandinavian countries. He's not what you might call an international authority, but he has been to Russia also."

"Lecturing?" asked Mason, his interest keenly aroused.

"No, that was in connection with arrangements for an art exhibition at the Glypotek Museum in Copenhagen. Socialist Realist art in the pre-war period."

An odd theme for an exhibition in Denmark, Mason thought, picturing gleaming tractors, rosy-cheeked peasants and acres of socialist wheat.

"That must have taken some doing," he remarked, imagining the logistics involved.

"He went several times to Leningrad," Helvi said, with evident pride. "There were lengthy negotiations with the

Russian authorities before they would let the paintings out. Security concerns, mainly."

"That's understandable."

"Uncle Paavo used to joke about it quite a lot."

"Did he travel alone to Leningrad?"

"In so far as I know," she replied.

"Did John Ormond go with him?"

"Of course not, Mr Mason. Why ever would you ask that?"

"Only because he was something of a Russophile too. Besides, he spoke the language, whereas your uncle did not."

"An interpreter was provided by Intourist," she explained. "An Estonian who spoke both Finnish and Russian."

"But do you know for certain that Ormond did not go along on maybe just one of those trips?"

"Why would both he and my uncle conceal that from me?" she asked, ingenuously.

"A fair question," Mason said, thinking they may well have had their own reasons. He began tapping nervously with his fingers on the table, wondering where he had seen before the bearded gentleman sitting half-concealed behind a copy of *Helsingin Sanomat*. Could it be the same individual he had noticed in this restaurant a few days ago?

"The Glypotek exhibition took place in . . . ?"

"In May," Helvi knew at once. "Early in May, for about ten days."

"How did your uncle travel to Leningrad? Was it by sea, by rail, by air?"

"He always traveled by car, along the coastal route via Kotka and Vyborg."

A broad grin suddenly lit up her girlish features, as she eyed the detective with a mixture of amusement and bewilderment.

"I think I can see what you're driving at," she said. "You are thinking that Uncle Paavo somehow spirited John behind the Iron Curtain!"

"Is that so improbable?" he asked, with a questioning look.

"Instead of reading fiction," she quipped, "you should write it. You have quite a vivid imagination."

Mason's features relaxed into a half-smile. She was evidently fully as skeptical of that proposition as Major Forsenius had been.

"Don't let me detain you further," he said. "It's a quarter to two already. You won't want to be late back at work."

Glancing again towards the bearded gentleman as they rose to leave the restaurant, he got only a partial view of his face, as he had on the previous occasion he had noticed him in this same restaurant sitting behind the spread pages of a Finnish newspaper. Was this someone, he wondered, who regularly took his meals at The Three Counts? Or was it somehow the very same person the *talomies* at the Kulosaari apartment had mentioned? He might almost have thought the man was shadowing him, except that on both occasions he had been seated at the same table by the time Mason arrived.

"An interesting word, *talomies*," he remarked to Helvi, always keen to improve his linguistic knowledge.

"*Talo* is Finnish for house," she explained pleasantly, just as they were parting. "And *mies* simply means 'man'."

"The man in charge of the house then," the detective said. "What we would call a janitor."

She repeated it a couple of times after him, glad to learn a new English word. He watched as she stepped briskly across the central tramlines to the far side of Mannerheim, before disappearing down a side-street by Stockmann's store.

CHAPTER SIX

L ATER THAT DAY George Mason found himself, at the special invitation of Viljo Forsenius, relaxing in the sauna at the major's country home several miles east of the city along the coastal route. Never in his life had he experienced silence as complete as that which now reigned in the Finnish countryside after dark, beneath the heavy snow-cover, through which the major had nimbly cut a path from the house to the bottom of the garden. Unlike the electric stoves in the city, this sauna was heated by wood, which they kept adding until the temperature rose above a hundred degrees, the minimum acceptable for a comfortable bath. Forsenius then sprinted back naked to the house to retrieve from the refrigerator the cans of beer he had overlooked. Left to himself for a few minutes in these rustic surroundings, Mason could not help but reflect that even the most unpromising assignment had its compensations; and this bath, as the guest of a native connoisseur, he regarded as a bonus.

The Finn soon reappeared and, agilely for his years, sprang up on the bench opposite the detective. Mason noted how well-preserved and physically fit his opposite number was for someone in his early fifties, contrasting the trim, athletic figure opposite him with his own increasing corpulence. For the Finns, physical culture was something of an obsession, running to such excesses as winter bathing through the ice of frozen lakes, rolling in the snow after sauna or setting off on marathon cross-country ski-tours. No wonder their athletes performed so well, in proportion to their numbers, at winter Olympics.

Forsenius leaned across to read the thermometer with studious concern. Then, apparently oblivious of Mason's presence, he stretched out full-length on the bench and closed his eyes; it was the traditional way of relaxing after a day's work. After a while, he roused himself and began ladling cold water over the smooth stones capping the stove, causing a rush of steam to rise up and then descend in tingling droplets on their bare skin. Motioning to Mason to do likewise, he then gripped a birch-switch and commenced flaying himself, filling the hut with the pungent aroma of birch leaves mixed with steam and sweat. Mason felt the blood course with renewed vigor through his veins and felt glad enough, considering the weighty problems on his mind, to abandon himself to the rigors of the bath and its twin disciplines of silence and endurance.

Half an hour later he emerged in the wake of Forsenius, with a better understanding of the Finnish custom of entertaining Russian diplomats all night in such surroundings, with respites for chilled beer and sausages grilled on the hot stones. The common sweat and spirit of camaraderie would make light of the knottiest problems, if they did not evaporate altogether in the heady atmosphere.

They took cold showers, scrubbed each other's backs, toweled thoroughly and donned warm dressing-gowns in the recovery room, at which point the major passed him two cans of beer.

"I liked the bit with the birch-switches," Mason said, gratefully quaffing the chilled liquor. "They didn't have those at the Kivi sauna."

"Only available in the country," Forsenius said. "It's good for the circulation. But take it easy with the beer. Alcohol takes quick effect after sauna and I hope you survive long enough to do justice to my wife's cooking. She is at this moment preparing supper."

"Your hospitality is greatly appreciated," Mason said, with a home-from-home feeling.

"Don't mention it," Forsenius said. "This is our customary way of receiving foreign guests."

"Did you come up with anything on Maxim?" His mind had been laboring through the last purgatorial half-hour or so to concentrate on business. Or could it be that the major regarded this as a purely social occasion?

"Nobody of that name has applied in recent years for a residence permit. The individual you have in mind is therefore here illegally or someone just passing through."

"What about Kilpinen?"

"Kilpinen?" repeated Forsenius, as if approaching the question from an immense distance, from the far side of some mental steppe or arctic tundra.

"Your vodka-runner, remember?"

"We checked on him too. He's had no subsequent problems with the authorities. Clean as a whistle."

"I'd stake half my pension he's somehow connected with Ormond's disappearance."

The Finn eyed him curiously, wondering if the sauna heat had not gone to his head.

"According to his niece, Paavo Kilpinen made regular trips by car to Leningrad around the time Ormond vanished."

"The same theory you advanced to me the other evening?" Forsenius asked, skeptically. "That Ormond was somehow substituted for Academician Tarkov at the Finno-Russian border?"

The detective nodded, while Forsenius sipped his beer thoughtfully and opened a second can. Eventually, he remarked:

"You have an interesting speculation only. Hardly a case. How, for example, do you connect Kilpinen with Tarkov?"

"I met with his niece for lunch earlier today. Her uncle is a strong admirer of Tarkov and is very familiar with his writings. He even owns a signed copy of one of his books."

"Interesting," Forsenius agreed. "It could imply that they met, perhaps even that they had a close association. Or it could simply mean that Tarkov did a book-signing session here at Academic Bookshop, the buyer of all imported books, around the time the Finnish edition came out."

"There are a lot of coincidences involved here," Mason pressed. "Too many, in my view, to be casual coincidences."

"What was Paavo Kilpinen doing in Leningrad?" the Finn asked suspiciously, as if his nose smelled vodka again.

"In connection with arranging an exhibition of Socialist Realist art at the Glypotek museum in Copenhagen."

"And you think he brought Tarkov out in one of the crates?"

"We should tackle Kilpinen himself about that," Mason said, ignoring the jibe.

"Pull him in for questioning? On what grounds . . . kidna pping? Come, Inspector, you are too old a hand for that. We could summon him to a meeting, but if he is implicated in any way that will only put him on his guard."

"Ormond *has* to fit the puzzle somewhere," Mason insisted, bringing down the palm of his free hand heavily on the wooden bench.

"You are sticking to the theory that Tarkov was physically exchanged for Ormond?"

"As I see it," Mason said, more calmly, "Ormond could have been a willing party to the whole scheme. Doing his bit for literature and freedom of expression. He was an idealistic young man, by all accounts."

"Weren't we all once?" Forsenius quipped, sardonically.

"In our individual ways," Mason said. He recalled how he himself had once taken part in nuclear disarmament demonstrations and almost got himself arrested.

"Then where do you suppose your compatriot is at this moment in time?"

"He could have gone underground inside Russia. Tarkov would have had many contacts among dissidents who would be willing to provide shelter. Leningrad is a large, populous city easy to disappear into, I should imagine."

Forsenius sipped his beer thoughtfully and offered his counterpart a small cigar. Mason gladly accepted, musing as he lit it on the difference between his present comfortable situation and the uncertain fortune of his compatriot. Fate was rarely even-handed.

"Let me propose to you an alternative theory," the Finn said, eventually. "Suppose John Ormond was not a willing party to this exchange. Suppose he was drawn into it—duped, if you like—by his interests in literature. Paavo Kilpinen could easily have set him up by promising him translation rights. He would then need to be eliminated, to tie up loose ends."

"That puts Uncle Paavo in a most unsavory light," Mason objected.

"Don't forget he has a record of alcohol smuggling."

"Vodka-running is one thing. Outright murder quite another. And where would that place Tarkov himself? Would he have been a knowing party to such a scheme?"

"The academician may not have known all the details. There would have been no need to tell him everything. There may even be other parties involved," the major went on. "More sinister forces than either you or I can imagine."

"Such as?" Mason asked, uneasily.

"Don't you think it possible that powerful interests could be using Tarkov for their own ends?"

"What sort of interests?"

"One need not perhaps look very far. The KGB, for instance, might very well have contrived the whole business, to disembarrass themselves of one of their most outspoken critics. With Tarkov out of the country, they could focus their attention on other, less high-profile dissidents."

Mason gazed back at the Finn in frank amazement. Such machinations would never have occurred to him, not in his wildest dreams. He had always prided himself, in fact, on the simple approach to detective work. People were predictable and you only needed to be a keen student of human nature to figure out how they would react in a given situation. Forsenius's notions took him way out of his depth.

"It sounds fantastic," he had to admit. "Yet you are much closer to the Russian way of thinking and dealing than I am."

"We have to consider all possible options," Forsenius said, "if we are going to get anywhere. Let us hope, for Ormond's sake, that your view is more accurate than mine."

"Paavo Kilpinen, in your model, ties in with the Russians."

"That's quite possible. On the other hand, he could also have been their dupe. We'll keep a closer eye on him. If he's mixed up in something, he's going to make a false move sooner or later. Helsinki abounds in contacts of the KGB. Some of them are well-known to the police, the smaller fish whom we allow a degree of operational freedom. And you, Inspector, what will your next move be, a trip to Leningrad?"

Mason scowled. "If only that were possible," he replied. "Neither my brief nor my budget extends to that. I'll get in touch with Chief Inspector Harrington in London, explain the situation to date and see what he suggests. If it's all becoming too political, he may want me to pull out."

"Don't give up now," the Finn observed, "after you've done so much useful spadework."

"My best instincts are to stay with the case. I feel I owe it to the man, to Ormond, I mean."

"Come," urged the other, encouragingly. "Let us go back up to the house. My wife Soili will have supper waiting. Chicken risotto, with asparagus tips."

"Sounds fine to me," replied the grateful Englishman, his appetite piqued by the sauna.

The two men dressed quickly, Forsenius returning briefly to the hot-room to extinguish the stove. Collecting their towels, robes and empty beer cans, they sprinted back up the pathway to the house. Fresh snow had already obliterated their former tracks.

*

Two days after his enjoyable evening with Major Forsenius and his attentive wife Soili, George Mason went to the British Embassy in the Brunnspark in the hope of receiving by diplomatic bag further instructions from Harrington. Foremost in his mind was the possibility that his superiors had decided to call off the investigation. On the other hand, there could be facets of this case which he knew nothing about. The service often acted on the principle of fragmented knowledge, only those higher up having the full picture. His assignment may only be a small part of something much larger. He had hinted to Harrington the direction his enquiries were likely to take and it would be for him to decide if Mason's continuing presence in Helsinki was going to be useful. He pictured his chief sitting comfortably behind his walnut desk in Scotland Yard, with regular servings of tea and the odd tot of his favorite malt whisky. What could he know of the rigors of an assignment like this?

Since lunch-time yesterday he had been confined to his hotel during a particularly heavy snowstorm which reduced even this capable city to a virtual standstill. He occupied his time writing a long letter to Adele and paying several visits to the hotel bar, where he had made the brief acquaintance of a young German journalist from Freiburg, snowbound in Helsinki on his return from Rovaniemi, where he had been gathering material for an article on the Lapps. They took breakfast together, watching the snowplows hard at work along Mannerheim and the trams clanking slowly up and down, before going their separate ways; the German hoping to reach Seutola Airport in time for his morning flight to Frankfurt, Mason taking the opportunity to fit in a little Christmas shopping as he made his uncertain way up the main street and briefly entered Stockmann's department store. He was particularly interested in the glassware and ceramics, for their original designs and colors that would appeal to his wife.

Harrington's reply, read between gulps of hot Embassy coffee, put a new emphasis on the case. The sensitive material Ormond was thought to possess was nothing less than a missing Tarkov manuscript! The link with the translator was so far merely circumstantial, since it had come to light through a defector from Tallinn that Ormond had some previous experience translating dissident Russian literature; something Arthur Greenwood was unaware of, or had failed to mention. Harrington stated the manuscript's original title, *Zapiski Tarkov*, as well as the presumed English version, *The Tarkov Papers*. There was no indication of the reason for the manuscript's importance. His chief would not want him to know too much, just to do the footwork necessary to retrieve the writings, if at all possible.

Leaving the Embassy, he began making his way down to Police Headquarters opposite South Harbor. A ship's siren pierced the wintry air and he slackened his pace to watch it approach the quay, its incisor-prow cutting through the harbor ice like a sharp knife through icing on a cake, sending up a spray of ice-particles as it berthed. He had to step back to avoid being showered. Having absorbed its contents, he took out Harrington's letter and lit it with the same match he used to light his first small cigar of the day, staying at the harbor long enough to watch the elaborate process of securing the vessel's hawsers to the capstans and the huge harbor crane come trundling along its rail-track to meet it, so that unloading could begin. Mason noted with interest the vessel's name, *Zyklus*, and its port of origin, Hamburg. A freighter of some kind, that would no doubt return to Germany with the sawn timber massively stacked on the quayside.

"It's the first I've heard of a missing manuscript," Forsenius said, as the detective confronted him in his well-heated office. "But from what you say, locating it is even more important than finding Ormond."

"The assumption in London is that they might both be found together, although the link is a tenuous one at the moment. There's no need, for now at any rate, to establish priorities."

"So the case is even wider open than it was before?" the major said.

Mason regarded him anxiously. "But I can still count on your full support?" he ventured.

"We shall of course give you any assistance you may need. But you must understand that, in view of our rather delicate relationship with our powerful neighbor, ours must remain the more passive role."

Mason sensed that his opposite number spoke to some extent with tongue in cheek. He was now well aware of the realities of Russo-Finnish relations, of the need to refrain from activities that might be construed as hostile. The Finns set great store on their viability as an independent state, in view of the fate of their ethnic cousins in Estonia and that of the other small Baltic nations, Latvia and Lithuania.

"I do have some news for you, however," Forsenius said, encouragingly. "Following our discussion in the sauna the other evening—by the way, Soili much appreciated your company. She loves London and valued your tips for visitors—I got in touch with Paavo Kilpinen. He offered to come down here of his own choosing. He knows something all right, but at the same time he sounded a little fearful. Thought you might like to be in on the interview; it's at 9 am tomorrow."

"The devil I would!" Mason exclaimed, elatedly.

"We'll see you then," Forsenius said. "Right now, if you'll excuse me, I've got to drive up to Porvoo, just north of here, to look into a case of suspected arson."

The curious life-style of John Ormond became a bit clearer to George Mason later that day when, following a second extended visit to the Hotel Kivi sauna and a leisurely evening meal at his favorite table at The Three Counts, he decided to drop by the Marlowe Club, the key haunt of expatriate Britishers living in the Finnish capital, which the missing translator was also known to frequent from time to time. By going early-evening, he had a better chance of catching the steward alone. Grant Ellison's name, together with the club's address, was the one piece of really useful information he had gleaned from the tight-lipped proprietor of the Polyglot Institute, an individual mainly concerned it seemed with the avoidance of scandal and its possible effects on his thriving business. If the Finns were bent on anything, it was gaining a fluent command of the English language.

He found the place easily enough with the aid of his street plan, on a quiet road facing Topelius Gardens. From the outside it seemed like an ordinary dwelling, part of an elegant terrace built in a more expansive era, the type of property most families could no longer afford to maintain and which now housed the headquarters of the less-obviously commercial types of enterprise, a medical practice, a Christian Science reading-room and the like. It came as no surprise to him on entering, guided by a lamp towards the rear of the building, that the ground floor was used for educational purposes. Judging by the play areas and the pervasive smell of plasticine, it was a kindergarten. Mounting the stairs, he was gratified to find himself in a very passable approximation to a London club, except that the Marlowe was not residential. He passed through a reading-room, glancing at recent editions of the London *Times, The Spectator* and *The Daily Telegraph,* and a billiards room where two elderly civil service types were engaged in a game of snooker, before reaching the small bar area. It was deserted save for the steward polishing glasses for the evening trade. Mason at once had the pleasurable sensation of being in familiar territory; it was as if he had entered an English pub, with a typically English barman in a plum waistcoat and bow tie, beer pumps and popular English beers such as Boddington's and Flower's. A portrait of the queen looked down benignly on the scene.

The steward, who was standing with his back towards him, turned as he entered.

"Grant Ellison?" Mason enquired, affably.

The man scrutinized him carefully, striving to recognize the detective's frost-piqued features.

"You a member here?" he asked, testily.

"Afraid not," Mason replied. "But we may have a mutual acquaintance."

"The Marlowe is strictly members only," Ellison said stiffly, not at all taken in by the detective's suave approach.

Mason did not mind. It was often the reaction of others to his presence, part of his aura as a policeman that over the years he had grown to accept. He produced identity.

"Scotland Yard?" exclaimed the other, taking a step back.

"George Mason, at your service."

The steward appeared slightly flustered, but soon recovered his customary poise.

"Welcome to the Marlowe Club, Inspector," he said. "What will you have to drink, on the house?"

"A Boddington's will do nicely," Mason replied, watching with approval the sudden tilt of the pump handle, followed by the steady gush of one of his favorite ales.

"Your very good health," he said, taking a large quaff to counter the after-taste of the salt-herring he'd eaten for dinner.

"This is a surprise," Ellison said, unsure whether to adopt a familiar or a deferential stance. "What brings Scotland Yard this far north?"

"I'm making some enquiries about a certain John Ormond, late of Strandweg, Kulosaari."

"Did you say *late* of Kulosaari?" His tone registered surprise.

"You didn't know he had gone missing?"

"Thought he'd returned to England," Ellison said. "But I must admit to being a bit put out that he did not wish me good-bye. I remarked on the fact to my wife at the time."

"When was the last occasion you met him?"

"Now wait a minute, Inspector. Just what is all this about?"

"As I explained, I am trying to trace Mr. Ormond. I understand he frequented this club."

"He's not in some kind of trouble, is he?" the other asked, guardedly.

The detective raised his glass before replying, savoring the satisfying tang of real ale before setting it back down on the bar.

"Difficulty is the word I would use, rather than trouble."

"The last occasion I met him?" Ellison said uncertainly, turning to the sink to turn off the faucet he had inadvertently left running. Mason felt confident of him. His background would have been thoroughly vetted before his appointment as steward in such a prestige club.

"Some event, perhaps, held here at the club during the spring."

"It must be more than six months ago, Inspector. My memory's not all that good."

"Take your time," Mason urged. "There's no hurry."

He ordered another pint, waiting until Ellison served two members who had just entered, a smartly-dressed young man and woman he thought might be Embassy personnel. His gaze followed them as they occupied a side table and engaged each other in friendly conversation. The place became even more like an English saloon bar, which suited the sociable detective. As he sipped his beer, his attention switched back to the steward. From his demeanor, one would almost have said he was a professional barman; yet that seemed hardly likely in a city of this size. More probably, he had a day-time job elsewhere.

"I understand you have a flourishing dramatic society," he remarked, indicating the framed photographs of well-known actors lining the walls.

"We stage two plays a year," Ellison said, proudly. "We're doing Ibsen's *Seagull* for our Christmas program this year. Why not drop by?"

"I doubt I shall still be here," Mason said, evasively.

"A pity," returned Ellison. "Christmas is very pleasant in Finland."

"You certainly have the right atmosphere for it. Have you lived here very long?"

"For fifteen years, on and off. I married a girl from Lahti and that made all the difference. Few foreigners stick it out here more than a few years. The climate gets to them, especially the winter darkness."

"I can understand that," Mason said, with feeling. "Did John Ormond like it here?"

"He seemed quite settled, as far as I could judge.'

"Was he part of the drama group?"

"No. But he did attend the productions. Everybody did. Come to think of it," he went on, in a flash of illumination, "our spring performance would, in fact, be the last time I saw him."

"You're quite sure of that?" Mason came back at once.

"Positive. I saw him being introduced to the outgoing ambassador, Sir Archer Penfield. Give me a minute and I'll check the exact date in the club diary."

He was interrupted momentarily by the entrance of an older couple who approached the bar to order gin-and-tonics. After greeting and serving them, he slipped behind a draw-curtain at the rear of the bar and re-emerged moments later with the club diary in his hand, opening it on the counter in full view of the detective.

"Friday, April 29th," he declared. "What a night that was. We did John Osborne's *Look Back in Anger*. Sir Archer seemed a bit put out, complaining about bad language and the permissive society in general. But he soon got over it, it being his last night here; and he was quite looking forward to his transfer to Athens."

"Did Ormond mix well here, with the Embassy types and so on?"

"He stayed round the bar, mainly," Ellison said. "The Embassy people tend to be a bit clannish. He preferred to talk to me about things we had in common, such as Coventry City soccer team and events in the English Midlands. We're both from that area and we bonded well."

"Did he ever express political opinions to you?"

"Only in an idealistic sort of way. The typical left-wing views of many university men, Third World issues, human rights and so on."

"Did anything he said lead you to think he might have communist sympathies?" Mason asked, reviving one of his favorite theories.

Ellison's features registered both incredulity and amusement. He paced to and fro in some agitation, rearranging glasses and hand-towels.

"You can't be serious, Inspector," he said, eventually. "John Ormond was as true blue an Englishman as any I've met. A decent Coventry lad, without a doubt. Why, I even knew his family back in the old days, before I moved out here."

"In connection with your job?" Mason enquired, to get the full picture.

"Electronics is my main field," Ellison explained. "My Finnish employers transferred me here from their plant near Wolverhampton.

Just then a large group of younger members came in, fully occupying the steward's attention. The detective transferred with his glass to a vacant table, retrieved the recent copy of *The Times* from the reading-room and spent an enjoyable hour in the convivial atmosphere of the club catching up on recent events in England, glancing across to the other tables from time to time to form a good impression of the club's regular clientele.

When he finally got up to leave, he returned his empty glass to the bar and said:

"Much obliged to you, Mr. Ellison. I appreciate your help."

"You're very welcome," the steward replied. "Now don't you go getting any wrong ideas about John. And try to make our Christmas production."

"Will do my best," Mason said, with more tact than conviction. Ibsen was hardly his cup of tea.

CHAPTER SEVEN

A S GEORGE MASON made his laborious way along Esplanade the following morning, to sit in on Major Forsenius's interview with Paavo Kilpinen, he turned over in his mind the significance of what he had learned the previous evening, that John Ormond had been in Helsinki as late as April 29th, one day after his birthday dinner with Helvi. That the translator had failed to turn up for work during that final week suggested to Mason that he was already caught up in the sequence of events leading to his disappearance. Or could it simply have been that Ormond had decided to take a week off work to attend to personal matters? He assumed that Arthur Greenwood was telling him the truth in claiming not to have seen him all that week; yet even his statements might be open to doubt.

He was half-way along this pleasant street fringed with snow-clad trees before he became aware of something unusual in the atmosphere of the city. The unexpected pleasure it occasioned temporarily pushed all other preoccupations from his mind. There was music in the air, coming in so far as he could judge from the central shopping area. Christmas music, reminding him that they were already into December, leaving little enough time to get this case cleared up by the end of the year. He recognized some of the tunes, appreciating a standard of musicianship far higher than the hackneyed carols relayed through English shopping centers at this festive season. There were ensemble pieces by Handel, Bach and Vivaldi interspersed with the choral singing, lightening his step through the heavy snow.

It was still with a sense of relief that he gained the interior of Police Headquarters, being blown almost bodily inside by a sudden gust of cold air from the open bay. The duty officer, recognizing him from previous visits, took his overcoat and hung it in an ante-room next to a huge cylindrical stove that went straight up through the ceiling to the floor above. A vintage, but nonetheless effective, form of central heating that would have been installed well over a century ago when the buildings were erected. He then rang through to the major's office, while Mason flapped his arms to improve circulation; one could freeze to death simply walking the streets in conditions like this.

"Do come in," said the major, heartily. "Don't believe you've met Paavo Kilpinen."

He completed the introductions, guiding the detective to a seat at one side of his desk before sitting down opposite his visitor, a tall gentleman with graying hair and typical Finnish features that bore only slight resemblance to those of his niece.

"Mr Kilpinen has just told me something very interesting," he continued. "We thought you should hear it too."

"You bet," Mason replied, eagerly. "Since I've braved so much snow to get here."

"The Inspector is having a little difficulty accustoming himself to our climate," Forsenius jibed. "But so far the weather has been relatively mild. In '78, for example . . ."

Mason winced at the thought, while Kilpinen smiled for the first time, a quick, nervous smile. He crossed and uncrossed his legs in quick succession, waiting for the major to resume.

"It seems there is something in your theory, after all," Forsenius said, appreciatively. "At least, in *one* of your theories. But only up to a point."

The detective beamed satisfaction. The news made his journey down here all the more worthwhile and he was hoping not to hear that Ormond had defected, the one theory he was more than ready to discount after speaking with Grant Ellison the previous evening.

"John Ormond does in fact tie in with Timor Tarkov, but not in the way you supposed," the major explained.

"You mean there was no substitution of one for the other at the Finnish border?"

"The academician's defection to the West was engineered by our friend here," he continued, glancing towards Kilpinen, who nodded gravely in agreement. "He was hidden in one of the crates of an art exhibition bound for Copenhagen."

"You don't say so!" Mason exclaimed. "Helvi told me about your frequent visits to Leningrad in the spring. I had a strong feeling all along that you were somehow involved. Your wise-crack the other day, Forsenius, about Tarkov coming out from Russia in a crate turned out to be remarkably on the ball."

"The exhibiton—Socialist Realist Art—received only cursory inspection at the point of entry into Finland," Kilpinen explained. "Tarkov might there and then have emerged from his concealment and claimed asylum, but his unannounced arrival on Finnish soil would only have caused embarrassment to our government, who were just then negotiating a delicate and, in some quarters, a very controversial defense treaty with the Kremlin."

"When the convoy passed through the check-point," Forsenius went on, "it proceeded to the Baltic port of Kotka, not all that far from the border. There, it drove straight onto the waiting ice-breaker *Tuuli*, bound for Denmark. Once the ship had left port, Tarkov emerged from hiding and enjoyed the freedom of the deck . . . and soon afterwards, the freedom of the West."

"That was quite an art consignment," Mason said, with feeling. "But I read in one of your newspapers recently that Timor Tarkov was now living in Switzerland."

"On arrival in Copenhagen," Kilpinen explained, "he was taken for a brief rest-stop to the country home of Hans Helstrup, president of the Danish chapter of P.E.N. International. After a few days there, he was flown to Geneva."

Mason glanced from one Finn to the other. For a former vodka-runner, Paavo Kilpinen evidently now stood very high in the major's regard; yet he still appeared ill-at-ease.

"Where does John Ormond fit into all this?" he asked.

"You were correct, Inspector, about the translation angle," Forsenius said. "Ormond is apparently in possession of the manuscript of *The Tarkov Papers*."

Mason looked at Forsenius, who in turn glanced at Kilpinen.

"I handed it to him personally, on my return from Denmark," Kilpinen explained.

"You also traveled with the crates?"

"Quite openly. The exhibition had to be under my constant supervision all the way. The Russian authorities insisted on that. Once it was installed at the Glypotek, the museum staff took over and I flew back to Helsinki with the manuscript."

"What date would that be, the day you arrived back in Helsinki?" Mason asked, to tie this new information into the general scenario.

"I arrived back here on April 25th," Kilpinen said, "and handed the manuscript to Ormond to begin the translation into English without delay."

"That could explain his failure to turn up for work during the whole of that week," Mason said. "But your niece said that the art exhibition was staged in early May."

"That is correct," Kilpinen replied. "It opened May 1st. The museum naturally required a few days in advance to un-crate it and set it all up. It was quite a large exhibition, over seventy paintings."

"So now we have a missing translator and a missing manuscript," Forsenius said.

Turning to Helvi's uncle, Mason said: "Why didn't you approach the police earlier with this information?"

"My initial reaction was that Ormond had gone into hiding to complete the translation," the other explained. "Other parties knew of the manuscript's existence and would be very eager to get their hands on it. But since he has failed to re-surface after all this time, I naturally grew very concerned and was on the point of contacting the police myself. Major Forsenius forestalled me."

The image of a bearded gentleman immediately flashed through the detective's mind and he recalled the strange, vaguely menacing phone call he'd received at the Havis Club.

"So where do we go from here?" Forsenius asked.

"Perhaps it would help," Mason observed, "if Mr Kilpinen could tell us everything he knows about John Ormond, to fill out the picture."

"Where to begin?" the antiques dealer said, rising from his chair and crossing to the window. A ship's siren pierced the frosty air.

"The morning ferry from Tallinn," Forsenius explained.

"John first visited us in the autumn of '78," Kilpinen said, with his back still towards them. "Shortly before the first snow. In fact, we had just returned from our holiday cottage on Lake Saimaa, which we had closed down for the winter. My niece Helvi, whom you have already met, knew him from the previous year, when she enrolled for an English summer-school in Vuokatti. She invited him to our apartment in Brunnspark the following year, after they met again by chance in Stockmann's department store."

"And the friendship continued from that time?" Mason asked.

"He became the friend of both of us. I took to him at once. He was rather quiet and self-absorbed, diffident even; but with a certain dry sense of humor, not unlike Finnish humor. Both Helvi and I liked him a lot. He began to visit regularly for dinner, once a week, to help us improve our English conversation. My niece also went with him to concerts and the theater, from time to time, usually when I was out of town."

"Did he have other friends here that you knew of?"

"I always assumed he had, among the established English community; but Helvi thought he was a bit of a loner."

"Did he ever mention to you someone by the name of Maxim?"

"In so far as I was aware, he knew no Russians here. Otherwise, I would not have negotiated the translation project for him. One has to be very careful in an open city like this. There are Russian agents everywhere."

"Did you thoroughly vet his background before offering him the work?" Forsenius wanted to know.

Kilpinen resumed his seat facing the major. "I saw no need to do so," he replied. "I thought I knew him well enough, and the Polyglot Institute has a good reputation in Helsinki. His association with them was sufficient recommendation for me."

"Yet your translator and your manuscript are both missing."

Kilpinen raised his hands in a helpless gesture. "I was really expecting the project to be finished by now; that John would have re-surfaced and I could take it to Tarkov's London publisher. What am I going to tell the distinguished academician?"

The two policemen fully appreciated his predicament and exchanged concerned looks.

"Tell him there has been some unavoidable delay," Mason suggested. "I'm doing my damnedest to solve this case. And I shall solve it, or my name's not George Mason."

His confidence seemed partially to revive the antiques dealer's spirits. The duty officer put his head round the door to ask if they required coffee and *pulla*, which the major then requested for three.

"Did it at any stage occur to you, Mr Kilpinen, that Ormond might have gone over to the other side and taken the manuscript with him?"

The dealer looked flabbergasted. "No, it certainly did not."

"But he did in fact, unknown to you, have Russian friends. Some time during April, he was given a copy of a well-known Russian novel by a person who signed himself 'Maxim'. Several people have told me of Ormond's left-wing views."

"It certainly is troubling to me that John knew some Russians."

"*One* Russian, so far," Forsenius corrected.

Kilpinen looked hard at the detective before saying: "Does having a Japanese friend make one a Shintoist?"

The major laughed out loud, while rising to receive the tray of coffees from the duty officer. Mason also managed a smile, taking the point with good humor. Refreshments were served and the atmosphere in the headquarters office became more relaxed and convivial.

"Come, Inspector," Forsenius said. "Enough of this line of reasoning. I expect John Ormond was no more a Red than you or I."

Mason was still determined to play devil's advocate.

"Perhaps I am better informed on the subject than you are, Major," he said. "I was speaking with the steward of the Marlowe Club only yesterday evening, about Ormond's political views."

"The what club?" the major challenged.

"The Marlowe. It's primarily a dramatic society for English expatriates over by Topelius Gardens. Ormond apparently had an aversion towards big business and the capitalist system in general, as a hang-over from his student days. He could quite possibly have been in league with the mysterious Maxim and duped you, Mr Kilpinen, into giving him an important dissident manuscript."

"Magnificent!" boomed Forsenius, rising from his chair and bringing his palm down hard on the blotter, so hard that his coffee spilled over into his saucer. "You should join a drama group yourself, without delay. Hercule Poirot, Miss Marple . . . you'd be in the right company!"

The antiques dealer looked on bewildered and not a little agitated.

"Is the notion so far-fetched?" Mason riposted, quietly.

"Pure conjecture," Forsenius observed.

"If you knew the real John Ormond," Kilpinen said, "I think you would change your view. He was in many ways a typical English liberal."

"Couldn't the same have been said of the celebrated Kim Philby, at least on the surface?" Mason commented, dryly. "Besides, if he'd gone underground to do the translation, don't you think he would have contacted you at some point, if only to report on progress? There's a lot more to this than meets the eye, including the fact that during his last few days in Helsinki Ormond kept to much of his usual routine, visiting his usual haunts, meeting the same people such as your niece Helvi. No one noticed anything unusual about him. Everything he did was entirely predictable, which suggests to me that he knew all along what his plans were at the end of that final week."

The two Finns exchanged uneasy glances, feeling there might be some truth in Mason's line of thought.

"Whatever *your* opinion of John Ormond is," Kilpinen said, coolly, "I will stick to mine. Don't forget that I'm the only one among us who knew him on a personal basis."

"And I," the major interjected, "for the time being will—as you English say—sit on the fence."

"What I should like to know," Mason said, "aside from whether or not Ormond made off with it, is what is all this fuss about a missing manuscript?"

The antiques dealer eyed him in disbelief. "*The Tarkov Papers* are of considerable importance to everyone living in the free world," he asserted, as if stating the obvious.

"And why is that?" Mason asked, leaning forward critically in his seat, hoping not to hear some mumbo-jumbo of ideology and cant.

"Because they advocate the complete dismantling of the present Soviet system of government and put forward very cogently the case for a free-market economy, freedom of the press and democratic elections to replace the one-party state."

"That's quite an agenda," Mason said. "In fact it's political dynamite."

"They will do their utmost to suppress it, which I fear may be the clue to its present whereabouts. It may well be in Russian hands, John Ormond along with it."

"Unless he personally handed it to them," Mason persisted.

"A possibility I am not even going to entertain," Kilpinen said, emphatically.

The detective shuffled his feet nervously on the thin piece of carpet, his eye attracted to the curiously irregular pattern only a Finnish designer could come up with. The major rose from behind his desk and crossed to the window, watching the sky brighten to the uncertain twilight that passed for day at this time of year.

"Haven't other works of Tarkov been published in the West?" Mason finally asked.

"Mainly autobiographical," Kilpinen explained. "In fact, I have a signed copy of one myself. *Echoes of the Steppes*. It is politically neutral, in common with much of his output. Tarkov was a distinguished member of the Academy of Letters, with an international reputation. The Russian authorities will feel doubly betrayed."

Forsenius turned from the window, checking his watch to indicate their time was up.

"The ball is now in your court, Inspector," he remarked, once again illustrating his excellent command of English idiom.

CHAPTER EIGHT

LATER THAT DAY, George Mason treated himself to dinner at the Havis Club. He chose a table towards the back of the dining area in order to observe the activities of his fellow clubbers without being too conspicuous himself. Ordering a beer, he took time to study the menu, so different from an English menu, stock items being reindeer, elk, trotters and salt-herrings. The ladies over on the far side of the dance-floor were already in place, sitting demurely by the thoughtfully-placed telephone receivers. Most of the men, at this comparatively early hour, were still at or near the bar. Ordering elk, with potatoes and red whortleberries, he found himself questioning again the attractions of the place for a young Englishman, feeling convinced that there was more than a casual connection between Ormond's disappearance and this bizarre enclave of Nordic night-life. He was also wondering if the mysterious caller on his previous visit had noticed his arrival and whether he would again offer him a piece of his sarcastic advice.

There was a fair amount of movement to and from the bar as the men began slowly to fill up the vacant tables, bringing their drinks with them. The same female trio continued to provide background music until eight o'clock, when the lights were again dimmed as the compere announced the first item of the cabaret. Rumanian Lulu, however, had moved on, possibly to venues even farther north, to offer exotic dancing to the Lapps; she was replaced by Natasha, a former ballet dancer from Sverdlovsk. Mason had seen it all before. He took the opportunity, now that the men's attention was riveted on the program, to scan the periphery of the club premises, the more obscure areas away from the bar and the dining-tables, to see if he could spot someone wearing a beard in a city of clean-shaven men. But he discerned no one of that description. Perhaps it was too early in the evening. He observed with an amused detachment the final flourish of what purported to be a dance of the seven veils and concentrated on enjoying his meal, his first-ever dish of elk. It was to his liking, if a little coarser than reindeer, the sharp bitterness of the berries providing the perfect foil.

When the lights went up, music for dancing followed. The telephone lines between the tables became suddenly busy and the men, surprisingly agile for their years, presented themselves with a formal bow to their partners of choice and led them onto the dance-floor. Few women remained uninvited, remaining passively with their drinks or chatting across the tables, fully confident that they would eventually receive an invitation. Mason found the whole process fascinating and slightly touching in a way. The human pursuit of romance recognized barriers of age no more than it did those of social class or nationality. He also noted that no woman there, in so far as he could tell, refused the offer of a dance; unless, of course, the suitor was too well-lit to stand up straight and present a stiff bow. The ladies were particularly strict on that score, as he had occasion to observe more than once during the course of the evening.

Since smoking was permitted, he lit a small cigar and ordered another drink. The trio began playing a tune he for once vaguely recognized, a change from what he took to be a medley of Finnish folk music. His fingers began automatically to tap the rhythm on the tablecloth.

"That tune they are playing," he remarked to the waiter. "Trying to remember its name."

The man smiled through the gap in his teeth as he set the fresh beer down on the table, pleased to be of service in such a small matter.

"A Calabrian folksong," he replied, knowledgably.

Mason realized at once where he had heard it before; it was in the après-ski lounge of an hotel in the Dolomites two years ago.

"Are they a resident group?" he enquired, indicating the trio of female musicians.

"The program changes every month," the waiter replied.

"I'm looking for a Russian gentleman named Maxim," Mason said, prompted by Forsenius's hint that it was probably someone passing through who had given Ormond a signed copy of *Quiet Flows the Don*. "He may have some connection with this club."

At the mention of the word Russian, the waiter seemed to draw back into an aloof professional posture. He shook his head negatively and moved on to the next table. Mason shrugged. It was worth a try, he thought, easing himself from his chair and negotiating his way carefully between the tables in the semi-darkness to visit the restroom. It was located in the foyer near the short flight of stairs leading down to street-level, an area decorated with signed and framed photographs of artistes who had performed at the club. After completing his brief errand, he paused to examine them. He recognized Lulu and Natasha at once, even fully clothed. Then, at the far right of the mini-gallery, he found himself gazing at the portrait of a bearded gentleman. He knew at once that he had seen this face before, even if partially hidden behind the spread pages of *Helsingin Sanomat* in The Three Counts restaurant.

He put on his reading glasses to decipher the scrawled signature beneath the photograph as best he could. The surname meant nothing to him, since it was written in Russian characters; but the initials *M. I.* were quite clear, being common to English and Russian. The middle letter would represent a patronymic, quite possibly Ivanovich. The *M*, at a shrewd guess, stood for Maxim. Maxim Ivanovich . . . , he repeated to himself, in a rare Eureka moment. His profession, as a touring artiste slipping in and out of the eastern bloc, would provide the perfect cover for any devious activities. If that was indeed him at The Three Counts it might imply that he was currently engaged to perform somewhere in this city, if not at the Havis Club.

He returned to his table in time for the commencement of the second part of the cabaret, a standing comedian whose jokes were solely in Finnish. The audience applauded warmly, while the detective, comprehending none of it, mulled over his recent discovery. It would be useful now if he could somehow come by information linking Maxim to this club during the early part of the year. The waiter, at first friendly, was avoiding eye-contact with him as he ferried trays of refreshments to his section of the restaurant. Since the bar area had gone quiet during the cabaret, Mason decided to approach the barman instead.

"Here on business?" asked the barman, obviously accustomed to foreign visitors.

"In a manner of speaking," Mason replied.

"What can I get for you? We have English beers."

"What I am really after is a souvenir program," he ventured.

"You a collector?"

"In a small way," the detective said. "I'm particularly interested in touring groups from East European countries. Their publicity material is very hard to come by in London."

"Natasha is leaving signed photographs as souvenirs," the barman said. "She's a first-rate artiste, at one time a leading member of the Kirov Ballet."

"Then I should very much like to have a copy."

"I'll slip into the back office while the bar is quiet and fetch you one."

Mason waited expectantly for the barman to return, conscious that he was a little too conspicuous in the well-lit bar area. When the man returned, he handed him the Natasha and a couple of past programs.

"The Vladimir Dance Ensemble performed here in the spring," the barman said. "They're also top-notch."

"Bit of a come-down for Natasha, wasn't it?" Mason asked, examining her picture.

"She was involved in a motoring accident; it ended her ballet career."

The detective thanked him and returned to his table. The comedian had departed and the room now had soft, revolving lights casting silvery freckles over the clubbers' faces. More intimate dancing ensued, his part of the room being practically deserted now that most of the men had made it firmly to the women's side. Thinking he would finish his drink quietly and slip out into the night, he was startled when his table phone suddenly rang. A woman's voice, gently coaxing, uttered a spate of Finnish too fast for him to understand.

"*Anteeksi,*" he said. "*En puhu suomea*—I don't speak Finnish."

"You English?" came back the dulcet voice, undeterred. "I speak very well English."

Quickly recovering his poise, Mason chuckled to himself at the bizarreness of the situation. He had not expected a woman to take the initiative.

"I think you are feeling lonely, English, sitting there by yourself."

"Whom do I have the honor of . . . ?"

"Table 17," came the prompt reply. "Just past the dance-floor."

Through the gloom and smoke-haze, he checked the illuminated cubes above each table until he espied a smartly-dressed woman with tightly-permed silver hair and large butterfly spectacles. He thought to himself: why not, indeed? A little female companionship, even if not of his own choosing, would help him relax and take his mind off more pressing matters.

"I'll be right over," he promised.

He rose from his place and negotiated his portly frame as best he could round the tight knot of dancing couples, before presenting himself with a stiff bow at the woman's table. At that moment, the music stopped and he found himself invited to sit down, feeling for the first time fully a part of Helsinki night-life.

"Virpi," she said smilingly, by way of introduction.

"George," he said, withholding his surname. "Can I offer you a drink?"

Before she could reply, her table phone gave a loud ring. Could she now have two suitors, he wondered, when moments ago there had been none?

"It's for you," she said, matter-of-factly.

He took the receiver from her, feigning not to notice her slender fingers linger momentarily against his own, and placed it close to his ear.

"Good evening, Mr Mason," came a faintly-mocking voice he instantly recognized.

"Who is this?" he asked, growing slightly agitated.

"My compliments. I see that you are fully enjoying the Finnish hospitality. Regarding our mutual acquaintance, Mr John Ormond, you may find him at Siltasaari."

The line clicked dead. Mason glanced round apprehensively at the sea of human faces, some serious, some sad; others happy, befuddled, beyond caring about the typical setbacks of everyday life. They seemed to mock him in his impotence as he turned first this way, then that in a vain attempt to pinpoint the location of his caller. The name Siltasaari throbbed through his brain. Was this individual taunting him, or offering him useful information?

"You look very concerned," his new companion said. "Is something the matter?"

"Just business," he replied. "Nothing very important. Now about that drink?"

Virpi's features relaxed into a half-smile. She was quite attractive, the detective thought, with those high cheekbones and dark eyes so typical of her race. A widow, most likely, who frequented the Havis Club perhaps to counteract feelings of loneliness or even to find a new mate. Why not enjoy her company for a while? It was not as if his caller had threatened him in any way and he felt no urgency to rush for the exit, as he had on the first occasion.

"Campari," she replied, amiably. "On the rocks."

*

On waking the following morning and glancing at his watch, he realized that he had overslept from the quantity of alcohol he had consumed the previous evening. Normally he drank little, just a few beers and occasionally a glass or two of wine; but the evening had dragged on in the company of the talkative Virpi and it had been past midnight when he finally got back to his hotel. As soon as he had showered and dressed he walked the short distance up Mannerheim for a late breakfast at The Three Counts. The day was clear and sunny for a change, with temperatures well below zero. There were few people about and motor traffic had subsided after the early-morning rush. Christmas music again filled the air, rising above the noise of the trams trundling along the oil-starved runnels. It was a pleasant-enough day to be abroad.

Settling down to a seasonal dish of rye-porridge and a strong coffee, he mused on the events of the previous evening, soon warming to the memory of his conversation with his female companion. Virpi had recounted to him, in very passable English, the story of her life. Now a widow, she had been married to an engineer employed in the control-room of a hydro-electric power-plant in the north of Finland. She herself had been a teacher at the local grade school. Following her husband's death, she had moved to Helsinki to be close to her two married daughters, and now occupied a small apartment on Lautasaari, another island suburb close to Kulosaari. The Havis Club, the National Theater and the several city-center cinemas were her main sources of entertainment. She expressed the hope that they might meet again in the near future, but he made no commitments. At the same time, he was pleased to have made another friend, in addition to the dapper major at police headquarters; someone in whose presence he could temporarily put aside professional concerns. Now these came again to the fore of his mind, as he reached inside his jacket pocket and drew out the past programs the Havis barman had obtained for him.

They were printed in both Finnish and Swedish, the two official languages of Finland, neither of which he could read fluently. As he was mainly interested in dates, the text did not greatly matter. He gave only a cursory glance at Natasha's program, whose photograph reminded him strikingly of the young Audrey Hepburn. The other two were more relevant. The first he examined was of an East German illusionist and his partner, *Manfred & Trudi*, who had appeared at the club in mid-July as part of their tour of the Baltic capitals, Tallinn, Riga and Vilnius. The remaining program was, as he had anticipated, for the Vladimir Dance Ensemble, as part of their tour of the Scandinavian capitals. The members of the cast were pictured on the inside and—no surprise—there was the bearded Maxim Ivanovich Slovotkin, his full name clearly printed, featured alongside his compatriots, two of either sex. More to the point, their engagement at the Havis Club spanned the last ten days in April!

That Maxim had met John Ormond on that occasion, George Mason was in no doubt. That he was now here in Helsinki, closely observing his movements seemed equally plausible to him. He instinctively glanced round the restaurant, focusing on customers reading newspapers, but drew a blank among the mere handful of people taking late refreshment like himself. He decided to telephone Forsenius without delay.

"News for you," he announced buoyantly, as the line became live.

"You've found John Ormond!" exclaimed the Finn, a strong tinge of irony in his voice.

"Not quite. But I do have a fresh lead."

"I'm listening. Do please elaborate."

"I think I'm on to Maxim. He's a member of a touring group called the Vladimir Dance Ensemble. They performed at the Havis Club in late April and may, I suspect, be in Helsinki right now, but at some other venue."

"That should be simple enough to check out," Forsenius said. "There aren't all that many night-spots here. And your translator is with him?"

"According to an informant," Mason declared, to test the Finn's reaction, "John Ormond is at Siltasaari. He could be holding out there, biding his time."

There was a long pause, almost as if the line had gone dead, before Forsenius said:

"Are you pulling my leg, Inspector?"

"Why?" asked Mason, with an uneasy feeling.

"Siltasaari is a cemetery. An island cemetery in the Gulf of Finland."

Mason shuddered inwardly. He was at a complete loss for words.

After a few moments' silence, the major said, more sympathetically: "Where are you now?"

"At The Three Counts, on Mannerheim."

"Meet me outside Stockmann's in half an hour. You're going to need skiing equipment."

Mason replaced the receiver, returned to the counter for a refill of coffee and a Danish pastry. He resumed his seat, feeling considerably shaken by the major's disclosure. Gradually, as he observed the Christmas shoppers milling about Stockmann's entrance just across the way, he began to take a more positive view of this startling development, his hopes rising that he would be back in London by Christmas. The prospect of a skiing expedition across the frozen Baltic to one of the islands in the archipelago, even on such a lugubrious errand, would provide welcome relief from trudging the snow-packed city streets, and it compensated in a small way for his vanishing trip to Italy. At the same time, he felt considerable angst over the fate of his compatriot John Ormond, that the trail should lead to such an abrupt end.

One hour later, clad in an anorak and ski-pants and sporting a new pair of cross-country skis and light boots chosen by Forsenius, he made his way with his Finnish colleague to a Volkswagen Beetle parked at the side of the department store. Three pairs of skis were strapped to the car's sloping back as it set off, with a scrunch of its winter tires, along the main thoroughfare to pick up the coastal road towards Kotka, the very same direction they had taken on the occasion of the major's sauna evening; and, if his memory served him well, the port of embarkation for Timor Tarkov aboard a timber freighter. Mason and Forsenius sat in the rear seats, to be driven by a junior officer, also clad in skiing gear. The major, lost in thought, said little until the vehicle was well beyond the city limits. The driver, taciturn as his race, concentrated on his task in the hazardous road conditions.

It suited George Mason, allowing him the opportunity to take in his surroundings. He watched the endless encroachment of forest on the one hand, broken now by a small farmstead with thin smoke rising from a chimney; or by a lake whose snow-covered surface withstood the tentative footfalls of an elk. On the other, there were frequent glimpses of the frozen ocean and the groups of islands often dotted with the small huts and cottages used by city-dwellers as summer retreats. It had been late morning when they set out, the sky lightening to something nearly resembling broad daylight, which would endure the few hours necessary for them to complete their task, before night descended again for their return journey. He was also content with his own thoughts and speculations on what sinister revelations might lie ahead. Similar preoccupations must have engaged the police major, who normally found plenty to say.

"Kotka," Forsenius announced, after they had driven for nearly an hour along a route which for the last few kilometers clung close to the shoreline, leaving the dense forest behind.

The black Volkswagen scrunched to a halt on the quayside. The police trio stepped out and stood for a few moments gazing across the bay, facing the brilliant sun suspended quite low on the southern horizon. The little timber port was quiet as a churchyard on this December day, locked in ice, with logs and sawn planks piled high on either hand, awaiting the spring thaw and the sturdy vessels that would ferry them to the old Hansa ports and beyond. The sea and the land were covered with the same white mantel, giving to both a uniform, synonymous character.

"Siltasaari," Forsenius said, his hitherto taut features breaking into a broad grin at the prospect of the physical exertion ahead. His junior colleague, with the physique of an Olympic athlete, set about unstrapping the skis and poles.

Mason followed the vague sweep of the major's arm towards the largest of the offshore islands, which effectively dominated the eastern approach to the bay.

"How far?" he asked apprehensively, feeling far less athletic than his colleagues, whose national pastime in winter was cross-country skiing.

"About a mile or so," the major replied, as if the distance were of small account. From his anorak pocket he pulled out a flask of brandy and offered it round. They then laced up their boots and slipped the toes into the metal clasps half-way along the light wooden skis.

"Thought you were an expert skier," Forsenius quipped, sensing the detective's predicament.

"Downhill," Mason answered sheepishly, "with the slope to provide momentum."

"This is far simpler. Just lean forward and push one foot after the other, keeping your skis parallel. Dig your poles in alternately for extra thrust."

Mason seemed skeptical of the value of the exercise.

"What can we expect to find?" he protested, "under several feet of snow?"

"Evidence," the Finn replied. "Isn't that what you want? Besides, if anything odd has happened here, the coastguard will be sure to know of it. This area is far too quiet for strangers to come and go unnoticed."

"Are you saying there's a coastguard out there in the middle of an ice-locked bay?" he asked, surveying the surrounding white inertia in disbelief, while helping himself to a second swig of brandy.

"It's his home after all," the Finn said, simply. "As we shall see soon enough, his house adjoins that of the cemetery superintendent. They both live there year-round. Keep each other company."

Without more ado, they set off down the slipway onto the frozen sea. The surface, however, was not so smooth as Mason had anticipated. It had frozen in ripples and wavelets that jarred against the skis and threatened to send them off at a tangent. Slowly, he got the hang of it. It was simple enough, just a matter of keeping one's balance while propelling oneself forward with arms and legs. Half-way across, the major paused to wait for him to catch up, sending the younger officer on ahead to announce their approach. Mason was soon out of breath, aware only of the seemingly large distance still separating him from mirage-like Siltasaari. A stiff breeze sprang up, blowing the surface snow like a fine powder into his eyes, nostrils and mouth, causing his cheeks to ache with cold. Bending almost double, he let his fur-clad skull take the brunt of the constant buffeting, felt the moisture from his breath turn to beads of ice on his chin. There were degrees of fitness, he reflected, noting the swifter progress of the Finnish police. And degrees of technique: that which was suited to the well-groomed pistes and ski-lifts of the alps, and that appropriate to sub-polar regions, to the vast, inhospitable wind-swept tundra and to the frozen ocean.

After the best part of an hour they were in the lee of Siltasaari, its snow-clad pines and spruces rising stolidly from the water's edge. For the first time they saw signs of human habitation, the coastguard's house and log cabins sturdy enough to withstand whatever the elements hurled at them. Thin smoke rose from the chimney above the open doorway where the junior officer was waving to them. Mason and Forsenius tilted their skis upwards against the slipway and were soon indoors thawing their limbs before the log fire. Any sneaking hopes the detective might have entertained that John Ormond would greet them in person were quickly dashed. The only two living souls on the island were the coastguard and the superintendent. The major exchanged small talk with them, mainly about weather, while Mason took in the details of the room, with its parquet floor covered with thick rugs and the simple wooden furniture typical of Finnish country homes. A keg of what he took to be illegally-distilled wood brandy stood by the hearth, seemingly unnoticed by the major, and the stuffed head of a wild boar glared menacingly at them from its mount on the wall.

The superintendent, a burly individual approaching retirement, eventually led them down a flight of steps at the rear of the building to a surprisingly modern small suite of rooms carved out of the bedrock. One of these, lined with filing cabinets and fitted with a large desk and swivel-chairs, served as his office; a second was marked SAUNA; the third appeared to be a workshop of some kind, with pieces of half-built furniture lying around, a trade that may have occupied the two residents during the slack winter months.

The official took down a large ledger from the shelf and spread it open on his desk for Forsenius to peruse. He examined the entries for the end of April and the beginning of May, reading the names out loud as if it were a roll-call of the dead.

"No mention of a John Ormond," he remarked, matter-of-factly.

Mason moved closer, to peer over his shoulder. After a few moments, he drew the major's attention to an entry for May 2nd.

"What do you make of that?" he said. "Plot 251: John Englander. Date of birth: Feb 14, 1952."

Forsenius gave Mason a quizzical look.

"It's the right age," Mason said, "and the date fits perfectly."

"You mean that John Ormond has been lying here all this while under a pseudonym? An intriguingly macabre touch to say the least. I should like to know who signed the death certificate."

"And the cause of death."

"We shall need a positive identification," Forsenius declared.

The official, who had so far taken only a bemused interest in the whole proceedings, immediately registered his concern.

"An exhumation will not be possible," he said, "until the spring thaw. The gravedigger does not return until May. The deceased are stored in the Kotka morgue until then."

"At least the body will be well-preserved," the major said. "But we cannot possibly wait five months. This is a matter of international importance."

"I should like to take a look at the plot," Mason said.

"If you think it will serve any purpose," the official observed. "The graves all look much alike at this time of year."

The small group left the office and remounted the steps to warm themselves again before the open fire. The coastguard offered them a tot of wood brandy, receiving in response a rather stern look from the major, who then produced his pocket-flask of cognac for a warming drink before they slipped outside to put on their skis. Following the superintendent's directions, they set off through deep drifts of snow towards the southern and windward side of the island, where the newest graves were situated. The junior officer headed back across the ice to turn over the Volkswagen engine in preparation for their return.

Locating the correct plot was more difficult than they had anticipated, since the recent snowfalls had obliterated paths and bearings. After a longish search they found it, marked not with a headstone or a cross, but with a short wooden stake bearing the plot number.

"It could be anybody lying here, for all we know," Mason said. "It could even be a former resident of Kotka."

"With a name like that?" the Finn countered. "All along this southern coast, the people are of unmixed Finnish stock. The same surnames recur with regularity. Swedish settlement—taking Englander to be a Swedish-sounding name—is much more prominent on Finland's west coast."

"So we definitely have an outsider lying here," Mason said, glancing wistfully out across the ocean.

"A non-native, certainly. But is it truly John Ormond?"

"The surname is certainly highly suggestive. But we must ask ourselves one thing, Major."

"And what is that?"

"If the opposition disposed of him in this way, why would they now decide to draw our attention to the fact?"

Forsenius gazed for a while at the heap of fresh snow. With a wry smile he observed:

"Because they may wish us to believe that he is dead, in the expectation that we would then close the case and you would return to London. They could then concentrate their efforts on locating *The Tarkov Papers*."

Mason glanced at his colleague in frank admiration.

"But why bury him under an alias?" he wondered.

"To bypass officialdom. They would need authentic documentation to inter the real John Ormond, including a death certificate signed by a licensed medical practitioner."

"An exhumation would be needed to settle the issue, but that can't take place for another five months. Can death certificates be forged?"

The major gave him an odd look.

"Forgeries do sometimes occur," he replied, cagily. "Mainly in connection with the theft of bodies from mortuaries. The forger may, for example, change the date of birth so that the corpse appears younger than it actually is."

"Why on earth should someone want to rejuvenate a corpse?" the incredulous Mason asked.

"Parts of stolen bodies often end up in human tissue banks. Even bones can be recycled for spare-part surgery, such are the advances in biotechnology. The younger the parts, the better the price they fetch."

"Unbelievable," Mason protested, "that such things could happen in a civilized society."

"People will stoop to almost anything where financial gain is the motive," Forsenius said. "But I suspect that, in this case, we may both be victims of a sinister practical joke. These individuals, whoever they are, could be playing some sort of game with us. Leading us a merry dance, as you say in England."

"Let us hope so," Mason replied, with feeling, "for John Ormond's sake."

"You don't mind being led on a wild goose chase?"

"More a snow goose chase, I would say," the detective wryly retorted.

They redirected their skis back towards the coastguard's house, where they partook of fresh coffee laced with brandy before the log fire, before setting back in the encroaching darkness over the frozen bay towards Kotka.

"If we do decide to open the grave in the spring," the major remarked to the superintendent before leaving, "we shall apply through the proper channels. Much obliged to you for your cooperation."

"My pleasure," the superintendent said, evidently relieved that the matter was closed for the time being, so that he could return to his carpentry.

"Come, Inspector," Forsenius urged. "We must press on. My colleague will be wondering what has kept us all this time. It will be well below zero on the ice, so don't freeze in your tracks. Keep moving forward, if only slowly."

Mason merely grimaced, gritted his teeth and set his face steadfastly ahead.

CHAPTER NINE

"**G**LAD TO SEE you've suffered no ill effects from your exertions of yesterday afternoon," Major Forsenius remarked, when George Mason arrived at Police Headquarters the following morning.

"Apart from a little stiffness, I'm fine," Mason replied, recalling with satisfaction the way they had crossed the bay in the dark, guided by the few shore-lights at Kotka.

"A sauna will soon sort that out," the Finn suggested. "But was it really all worthwhile?"

"I gave the matter a lot of thought over dinner," Mason said. "What strikes me as very significant is that Maxim and the Vladimir Dance Ensemble completed their Scandinavian tour at around the same time that the translator disappeared. It seems an even bet to me that they left Finland together."

"You mean that they were acting in collusion?"

The detective nodded.

"I definitely think you are onto something with this Maxim fellow," the major said. "The coincidence of dates is very compelling. But if they were acting in collusion, how do you account for yesterday's episode?"

"We are dealing with a very cunning and determined opposition," Mason observed. "The plot on Siltasaari could simply be a convenient way of 'burying' the old John Ormond in the event of any enquiries coming too close to the truth. The name John Englander is sufficiently suggestive of the real person, while at the same time introducing an element of uncertainty and mystery. But in my view it is a contrived mystery. Given a new name and a fresh identity, the translator, having acquired the manuscript of *The Tarkov Papers*, could be living a new life across the border."

Forsenius rose from behind his desk and crossed to the window, to observe the arrival of the morning ferry from Tallinn, whose siren pierced the frosty air.

"So we're now back to your original theory," he wryly remarked, turning to face the detective again. "An exhumation could prove you very wrong. Suppose we were to dig up the real John Ormond next spring."

"That's a chance I shall have to take."

"And what do you imagine this Maxim, whom you now claim is currently in Helsinki, is up to?"

"Keeping an eye on us," Mason proposed. "Making sure he feeds us all the wrong leads."

"Maxim I. Slovotkin," the Finn mused, half to himself. "The name doesn't ring a bell."

"It could be a stage-name," Mason suggested, as helpfully as he could.

"A secret agent will also have some sort of code name too. Help yourself to coffee and *pulla*," he offered, crossing to the filing-cabinet, "while I dig out some files."

The detective did as he was bid, serving himself from the tray on the major's desk. Forsenius began tapping with his fingers on the top of the cabinet, humming a tune in accompaniment, which Mason took to be from a tone-poem by Sibelius. Chief Inspector Harrington had a similar mannerism, he reflected;

a kind of off-key whistling when he has preoccupied, or when he felt he was definitely onto something.

"Would you recognize Maxim if you saw him?" the major asked, placing two buff-colored folders on his cluttered desk.

"Positive," Mason replied.

"These are from our rogues gallery." Opening one of the folders, he spread the contents before his visitor. They were single-sheet reports, some with a passport-type photograph at the head. "Take a peek for yourself. See if you recognize anybody."

"Who are all these individuals?" Mason asked skeptically, between mouthfuls of fresh *pulla*.

"This particular folder is headed SUSPECT ALIENS," Forsenius explained. "Persons known to be involved in irregular activities, alongside those previously convicted of a criminal offense. You may even have met one or two of them yourself, in the course of your professional life."

The detective examined them carefully. After a while, he said:

"The only one I recognize is Silvano Bondi. He did time at Wandsworth Prison some years back, for grand larceny. What on earth is he up to here?" he enquired, unable to read the Finnish text.

"Currency smuggling," Forsenius said, matter-of-factly. "Between Helsinki and Tallinn."

"Tallinn?" queried Mason.

"The capital of Estonia, just across the Gulf of Finland. A popular tourist destination over the last few years. Estonians are our ethnic cousins."

"Nice of you to visit them."

"Many Finns have relatives living there, whom they have not seen for decades. Opening their border to tourism earns them valuable foreign currency."

"Western currencies, particularly US dollars, will fetch a high price on the black market," Mason suggested, handing the material back to the Finn.

"Hence our interest in the likes of Signor Bondi."

"Your rogues gallery does not seem to include our friend Maxim, unfortunately."

"You have no positive means of identification?"

Mason reached inside his jacket pocket, drew out the program for the Havis Club and handed it across to the Finn, who scrutinized it carefully.

"The bearded gentleman in the middle, I presume," he said. "The one dressed as a Cossack."

The detective nodded.

"The features are not very clear from this photograph," Forsenius said. "We could have it enlarged, if that would help."

"I have a vague impression of him from The Three Counts," Mason said. "A clearer likeness would certainly be very useful."

"You do realize, don't you, that we could not pull him in unless he broke some Finnish law."

"But you could have him watched," the detective suggested.

A rather sly smile began to play round the corners of the major's mouth. Replacing the folders in his cabinet, he said:

"We may in fact already have something on him. Just a hunch, mind you, as you English say. Before we set off on your expedition to Siltasaari yesterday—my first skiing trip of the season, by the way—I had it from a reliable source, from the chef on board the *Lebed*, that there was a top agent over here in the spring. His code name is Lynx and he has the rank of colonel."

"The *Lebed*?" Mason asked. "That would be a Russian vessel?"

"Of the Red Star Line. It's a passenger ship on the Leningrad to LeHavre run."

"That's the very same vessel," the detective recalled, "that took the Vladimir troupe back to Leningrad. I checked the manifest with Finnish Tourist Agency. It called here on May 3rd."

"Time enough to bury John Ormond on Siltasaari, either literally or metaphorically," the major remarked.

"So Maxim Ivanovich and the Lynx could be one and the same person.?"

"It's an interesting possibility, certainly."

"Tell me more."

"That's all I know for the present; all my informant was able, or willing, to tell me, apart from the fact that Lynx operates in several West European capitals."

"The Vladimir Dance Ensemble provides the perfect cover, as I said before. But what would the likes of John Ormond be doing mixed up with a top Russian agent?"

"That is for you to discover," Forsenius replied, disarmingly. "Your only link between them is a signed copy of a novel."

At that point the telephone on the major's desk gave a loud ring. Forsenius lifted the receiver and listened attentively for a few moments. Then, with raised eyebrows, he looked pointedly at his visitor.

"The Vladimir troupe are currently engaged by the Workers Theater in Lahti," he said, dead-pan.

"Lahti?" enquired Mason, uncertainly.

"A small town about thirty miles north of here, noted mainly for its brewery."

"You don't say so! That would explain his presence at The Three Counts, if it's really him."

"I'd watch your back from now on," the Finn observed. "These people mean business."

*

Arthur Greenwood was teaching class when George Mason arrived at the Polyglot Institute later that morning, digesting on his walk from South Harbor Forsenius's confirmation of something he already knew, that Maxim Ivanovich was currently operational in Finland. As a member of the dance troupe, he would be here on a legitimate visa and there was nothing either he or Forsenius could do about it for the time being, since they had nothing more than suspicions to go off. Mrs Virtanen, the secretary, received him courteously, showed him into the private office he was already familiar with and bade him take a seat. He declined her offer of refreshment. The picture on the wall calendar had changed with the month, to give a view of the famous ski hotel at Pallastunturi, in northern Lapland.

How remote it looked, he thought, the solid timber structure nestled amid huge drifts of snow and silhouetted against the setting sun. Nature in the raw, unknown perhaps anywhere else in Europe. There would be nothing at all of modern paraphernalia just off the picture; no filling-station, no funicular railway, not even a ski-lift. The reindeer would be in their winter pens, leaving only the native fauna, the wolverines, arctic foxes, lynxes and hares to leave footprints in the pristine snow. It was an awe-inspiring thought.

The office door suddenly opened to admit the proprietor.

"Inspector Mason again," he exclaimed, in surprise. "To what do we owe this pleasure?"

That was something about the man which irritated the detective: his patent insincerity, which was why he did not fully trust him.

"Just routine enquiries," Mason said, noting that Greenwood did not offer his hand as he rose to greet him.

"What's the problem this time? Another missing Englishman? Afraid I can't help you there. Our remaining employees are all female."

"So I had observed," Mason said dryly, withdrawing the Havis Club program from his pocket and noting the very perceptible narrowing of Greenwood's eyes and his almost defensive look. "The small print at the foot of the page states: *Printed by Palvelu OY, for Polyglot Institute Language Services.*"

"That's correct," the proprietor said, recovering his sang-froid. "We have a successful small line of publishing services for theater and club programs, hotel brochures and general tourist material. It developed logically out of our translation business."

"This particular program," Mason said, "did it require translating?"

Greenwood took it from him and quickly scanned the text.

"It most certainly did. The Russian authorities provided the short biographies of the members of the Vladimir Dance Ensemble, for us to put into Finnish and Swedish. We then had the program printed for the Havis Club by Palvelu OY in Kotka."

"Kotka?" Mason queried at once.

"A timber port just along the coast. About an hour's drive."

The detective was on the point of mentioning his minor expedition there the previous day, but something held him back.

"John Ormond, as your only Russian expert, would have had a hand in the translation work?"

"John would have translated from the original into Swedish. Mrs Virtanen would have worked from that to provide the Finnish version."

"The leader of the Vladimir troupe, it states here, was Maxim Ivanovich Slovotkin."

"That is correct," Greenwood replied, as neutrally as he could.

"Did you ever come in personal contact with him?"

The proprietor was a bit hesitant, Mason considered, in his reply. In fact, he did not reply at all. He merely shook his head as he commenced officiously sorting papers on his desk.

"I have a class starting in a few minutes, if you'll excuse me," he said.

"Were you aware that Ormond and Maxim were friends?" the detective asked, abruptly.

Greenwood dropped his bundle of papers in complete surprise.

"What on earth makes you say that?" he exclaimed.

"I have my sources of information," Mason said, unwilling to lay all his cards on the table. "Did they meet in this establishment?"

"They most certainly did not. As I explained before, all translation work from the Russian Embassy arrived here by special courier."

"Then how do you imagine that they met?

"If you are insisting that they met," the other said, testily, "the most likely venue would be the Havis Club itself. Ormond, I gather, was a fairly frequent visitor there year-round. It's quite possible that, having translated the program, he made an effort to see the show. It's also quite likely, since he knew Russian, that he spoke afterwards with members of the troupe. Anything beyond that kind of limited contact would be very difficult to imagine, since members of those touring acts are expressly forbidden to fraternize with foreign nationals."

"For fear they might defect?" Mason asked sardonically, aware that Maxim and the Lynx were one and the same person and wondering if Greenwood knew that. Too much in this baffling case seemed to center on the Polyglot Institute for it all to be dismissed as mere coincidence.

"Defections by touring artistes of various kinds, ballet dancers, musicians and so on are not all that rare. You know that as well as I do, Inspector Mason. Now you really must excuse me," he said, opening his office door to let his visitor out, "or I really shall be late for class."

"We'll be in touch," Mason promised, exchanging a friendly greeting with the secretary, Mrs Virtanen.

*

Seeking a change from The Three Counts as a lunch venue, he decided to drop by the buffet at the main station. The concourse proved one of the more agreeable places to be on a winter's day, being very much like a covered street, with boutiques and restaurants well-screened from the platforms. As he sat ladling French mustard on the appetizing hot dogs the Finns call *nakit*, he reflected on what a cool customer Arthur Greenwood was. He quite evidently resented Mason's arrival on the scene, and it was at least an even bet that he was up to his neck in this affair. Pinning him down, however, seemed about as likely as finding a golf ball in a snow-covered bunker. Finishing his snack and lighting a small cigar to smoke with his coffee, he noticed something which had so far eluded him on previous brief visits. The platform at the far end of the concourse was the point of departure for the Leningrad Express. From where he was sitting he could just make out the line of dark-green carriages, whose windows were all curtained. There was nobody either approaching or leaving it; it simply stood there secretively, almost anonymously. A glance at the train indicator showed that it wasn't due to depart until early evening, which might well explain the lack of activity. He found himself wondering what sort of people made the trip on this daily service, to arrive at the Finland Station, Leningrad just as Lenin himself had done in 1917. Nor did it escape him that it was another possible route for the missing translator to have taken.

He ought really now, following Harrington's clear instructions, to concentrate his efforts on recovering the manuscript. Forsenius's confirmation of Maxim's presence in the area and their curiously inconclusive expedition to Siltasaari strongly indicated that, as he had begun to suspect, there were other parties keenly interested in locating *The Tarkov Papers*. Translator and manuscript may not, after all, be found together, justifying the two Kilpinens' and Ellison's assurances that Ormond would never have defected with it. If he had, it would now be safely lodged in the musty files of Russian bureaucracy.

There would also not have been those curiously cryptic and rather sarcastic phone calls over the love-lines of the Havis Club, the detective mused, as he watched with interest a long line of young schoolchildren clad in anoraks and

brightly-colored ski hats form loosely at the barrier to Platform
4. A glance at the indicator told him that they were bound for
Rovaniemi, the capital of Finnish Lapland, the jumping-off
point for the fells and ski-stations farther north. It brought the
Dolomites back to mind and the ever-receding winter sports'
trip he had promised Adele. The gate opened and the children,
holding their skis aloft, jostled each other in their eagerness to
board the train for the northbound journey of, Mason estimated,
at least ten hours. Their teachers would have their work cut
out, so excited did their charges seem.

His eye wandered back to the end platform, to the curiously
impersonal Leningrad Express. Now there was a Finnish
soldier, dressed in a gray ankle-length greatcoat with matching
fur hat, standing guard by the gate. Perhaps, he thought, they
were about to begin loading it with mail and packages before
its scheduled departure. Security would no doubt be at a
premium for a transit of this type. It would pull out of the station
silently, he felt, without so much as a whistle and pick its way
with smooth efficiency through the inner suburbs, the small
dormitory towns and rural villages until it became virtually
indistinguishable against the backcloth of pines and spruces
as it picked up speed through the vast stretches of virgin forest
that lay between Helsinki and the Russian border. He would
have given a month's salary for a trip on that train, wondering
if one could simply purchase a return ticket right here at the
booking office.

CHAPTER TEN

ABOUT THE SAME time that George Mason was finishing his lunch-snack at the station buffet, a bearded gentleman refolded the pages of *Helsingin Sanomat*, rose from his place at a corner table and returned the broadsheet to its rack before leaving The Three Counts restaurant. Once outside, he hailed a cab and within minutes stepped through the side entrance of the Hotel Kivi. He had suggested this quiet, back-street venue for his luncheon appointment with the proprietor of the Polyglot Institute, not least because the dining-room specialized in lake fish such as turbot and salmon-trout and boasted the best wine cellars in this northern city. On his free days from his engagement at the Lahti Workers Theater, Maxim Ivanovich liked to indulge his taste for haute cuisine.

Arthur Greenwood was already seated at a table for two, awaiting his arrival. Rising to greet the dancer, he shook his hand warmly. They then sat down and studied the menu with all the attention of professional gourmets.

"What's on special today?" the Russian enquired, optimistically.

"Baked arctic char," Greenwood said, with enthusiasm.

"Fresh or frozen?"

"Frozen, I'm afraid. Those northern lakes will be under two feet of ice at least by now."

"In that case," the other said, "I think I'll opt for the stuffed turbot. The Kivi chef has a contract with the locals at Lake Oulu for year-round fresh supplies."

"Fishing through the ice," Greenwood observed, "sounds a very laborious technique."

"But it provides a useful employment," Maxim remarked, "in the slack winter months."

The waiter came and took their order for the fish and a bottle of Muscadet.

"My thanks for your tip-off about that flat-footed Inspector Mason," Maxim then said. "I've been keeping tabs on him as best I can on my free days."

"Quite a turn-up," the proprietor said, "for a member of Scotland Yard Special Branch to arrive in our midst."

"Do you think he's after the same thing we are?"

"Hard to say at this point," Greenwood said. "He has only ever quizzed me about John Ormond. Never mentioned the manuscript. Do you really consider that Ormond, wherever he now is, is actually in possession of *The Tarkov Papers*?"

"We are pretty sure that Academician Tarkov did not have it when he arrived at the home of Hans Helstrup in Denmark. Our agent in Copenhagen was pretty confident on that score. We must therefore assume that he parted with it before embarking on the *Tuuli*. Going by what you yourself said, that Ormond was the only competent translator from Russian living in Helsinki, it seems the safest bet that the translation was entrusted to him, most likely at Kotka."

"But nobody knows where Ormond is."

"I think I can safely say," the agent said, "that I've thrown Mason completely off the trail. We managed to bribe the superintendent at Siltasaari to make a bogus entry in his records. It took a fairly hefty bribe, mind you. Mason took the bait and headed off down there, where he was directed to the appropriate plot. If he gives up on Ormond, he may well return to London. It's nearly Christmas after all."

"I wouldn't count on him doing that," Greenwood said. "He struck me as a rather tenacious, obdurate sort of chap. Must be high priority in London for them to send in the Special Branch."

"That's what makes me suspect they know about the manuscript and its significance to the West. It's political dynamite. Mason may even lead us to it. We have no idea at all where it resides at this point in time."

"Let Mason do the leg-work for you?" Greenwood said, as the waiter placed their appetizing dishes before them. "Very astute, Maxim Ivanovich. Very astute of you indeed."

They raised glasses and toasted each other, before occupying themselves fully with the enjoyable task of tackling a fine lunch. The proprietor gave the Lynx an occasional surreptitious glance, a look of admiration at his cunning and resourcefulness. Pushing his plate to one side after he had finished his meal, he said:

"I understood you actually met John Ormond earlier this year."

"He attended my performance at the Havis Club in April. I met him in the bar afterwards and, as we got along quite well and he seemed keen on practicing his Russian, I invited him for lunch at the little French restaurant near the university. Forgotten its name."

"The Alphonse?" Greenwood suggested.

"That's it," replied Maxim. "As he also seemed very interested in Russian literature, I bought a copy of Sholokov's *Quiet Flows the Don* at the Academic Bookshop—they have a very good Russian section—and gave it to him. He seemed very pleased and we went on to discuss a range of Russian authors. But when I mentioned Timor Tarkov to him, whose autobiographical writings are popular in the West, he appeared to freeze for a few moments and then abruptly changed the subject. Started on about skiing in the fells of Lapland."

"That's interesting," the proprietor remarked. "Did it arouse your suspicions?"

"Before leaving Helsinki on May 3rd, I went through his apartment at Kulosaari on the off-chance I might come across something connecting him with Tarkov. According to an accomplice of mine who had been watching his place, he had not been back there for several days. May already have gone AWOL by then. The manuscript trail has been completely cold ever since, which is highly significant in itself."

"Then let us hope he shows up, so that you can get to him before Mason does."

"If he should contact you, as his employer, at any point, let me know at once. My engagement in Lahti terminates at the end of this month, which does not leave us very much time. I shall then have to return with my troupe to Leningrad."

The language school proprietor then settled the bill and the two diners went their separate ways.

George Mason returned to his hotel room that same afternoon to find that it had been thoroughly gone through. The contents of his drawers were scattered across the carpet, his spare suit and clean linen lay in crumpled heaps on the bed. Even his laundry, which he had been stacking to take to the launderette, had been sorted. It was at times like this that he appreciated the value of traveling light; all he had with him were two medium-sized suitcases for a few weeks' stay. It was the psychological effect, more than anything else, which was so dstressing. A textbook break-in, of which he had investigated many in the early part of his career before his transfer to Special Branch; yet something he had never imagined happening to himself.

His main concern was for his pills, the two small phials he kept in the bathroom cabinet, which he considered essential for the efficient working of his heavy frame. One phial contained vitamins, which could easily be replaced at a local pharmacy; but the other held a special prescription from his own doctor to regulate cholesterol. It was imperative that he find them. A break in his medicinal regime could undo months of patient work. Having overcome his initial sense of shock, he searched through the drawers and went down on his hands and knees to look under the bed before discovering both phials, partially emptied of contents, in the waste-paper bin. With a sigh of relief, he collected the spilled portions and replaced them securely in their phials, cursing aloud the mindless intruder. He then rang reception to order hot tea to settle his nerves.

Relaxing on the bed after tidying up and replacing his effects, he fell to wondering who could have performed such a desperate act, risking discovery in broad daylight. If Maxim was behind it, there were interesting implications. It was the first time the opposition had shown a direct hand, apart from those curious phone calls at the Havis Club; and it may mean, rightly or wrongly, that he was one step ahead of them. Did they imagine he had *The Tarkov Papers* stashed away in his bedroom? Or some clue to its whereabouts? If so, they were even more painfully wide of the mark than he was. That thought gratified him as he sipped his tea, helping overcome feelings of defeatism which, uncharacteristically, had begun to beset him of late, particularly since his fruitless trip to Siltasaari. Or could it be that he was in possession of some talisman whose latent significance he was as yet unaware of himself? He racked his brain to think what that could be and revisited in his mind all the evidence he had so far gathered, unsubstantial as it seemed.

The intruder must have known that he was out. Either he was watching his movements or he had an accomplice on the hotel staff. The latter possibility was quite disturbing, for it meant that his every move was being closely vetted: what time he rose in the morning, when he went out on business, when he took his meals. On reflection, he inclined against that view. An insider would have done a tidier job, leaving little trace of his sinister errand. The intruder's motive might, at least partially, have been to alarm him, to put him off pursuing the case. If that was so, he did not know George Mason. It occurred to him to ring Major Forsenius, but there seemed little point having the police go through his room looking for fingerprints, since nothing appeared to be missing in so far as Mason could tell.

Rising from the bed, he crossed to the door to examine the lock. It had not been forced. Whoever had entered had evidently been able to pick the lock or had a spare key. On turning, he noticed Ormond's pocket-diary lying face-down on the floor beside the bed. It must have slipped from his jacket, he thought, when he was salvaging his pills. He stooped to retrieve it, glad at least that he had not lost it, and went through the entries he had already checked off. In addition to Helvi and the Marlowe Club, there were the names of several former girl-friends and that of an old business associate in Turku. They had already been eliminated from his enquiries. A green slip of paper then dislodged itself from the back of the diary and fell noiselessly onto the carpet. He picked it up and crossed to the window to examine it more closely in the fading daylight.

It turned out to be what he had always half supposed it was: a theater ticket; which was why he had not given it more than a casual glance on previous perusals of the diary. It was no ordinary ticket, such as one might purchase for the National Theater in Helsinki or the Workers' Theater in Lahti. Across the top were the words MALY TEATR, which the detective recognized at once as the famous Leningrad venue for contemporary opera and ballet. The ticket was for a performance of the ballet *Tsveti* by Dmitri Shostakovitch, to be performed by the Kirov Ballet. It was two years old, too long ago to be of any current significance. Maybe Ormond had kept it for sentimental reasons, the way some people kept sports' memorabilia. It showed at least that the translator had made excursions across the Russian border, perhaps by road along the Gulf of Finland; and it confirmed what Greenwood had told him of his employee's strong interest in Russian culture.

As he refolded the ticket he noticed for the first time a sequence of figures penciled on the reverse side, so faintly that they had almost faded, which explained his failure to register them before. He repeated them one by one to himself: 650341.

Curious, certainly; but what, if anything, did they signify? Helsinki telephone numbers had six digits, but the unbroken sequence did not immediately suggest that explanation. He moved to the bedside table and wrote 65-03-41 on the hotel notepaper provided for guests. Now that it really looked like a telephone number, George Mason was half-convinced that it was. The question now arising in his mind was whether he should dial it and, if he were to do so, what sort of response would he get. He rose and crossed to the window. It was mid-afternoon and already quite dark. The city workers would start heading home at four o'clock; not much point ringing now, better to wait until a bit later, when people could be expected to be in.

Satisfied that everything in his room was now in order, he went downstairs to the hotel restaurant, thinking it was overdue for a visit. He ordered the best approximation they had to afternoon tea: a flask of hot water, a selection of tea-bags and two thick slices of *pulla* with strawberry jam. By a stroke of good luck, the newspaper rack contained, among the Finnish broadsheets, a current edition of the London *Times*. Glad of the opportunity to catch up on some more recent news from England, and glancing round the half-dozen occupied tables to make sure no bearded gentleman was sitting half-concealed behind a copy of *Helsingin Sanomat,* he occupied a pleasant hour reading the news items and articles, even the leaders he normally skipped, before checking the prices of his small portfolio of stocks in the Business Section. There was nothing of particular relevance to his profession, apart from the usual catalogue of homicides, swindles and burglaries. Nothing involving Scotland Yard and his truculent and demanding superior, Chief Inspector Harrington, God bless him.

He returned to his room over an hour later in a much better frame of mind from his brief re-immersion in English affairs and the timely light refreshment which would tide him over until dinner. Everything in his room was as he had left it and the pocket diary was safely tucked in his jacket. He paced the room for a while, perfectly aware that this was going to be a long shot, before he commenced dialing the sequence he had copied onto Marski notepaper. After a brief interval the line became live.

"I'm calling with regard to John Ormond," he declared, as confidently as he could.

"I beg your pardon?" returned a female voice, having some difficulty with the foreign-sounding name.

Mason repeated the name more slowly.

"Are you sure you have the right number?" the woman asked, a little agitated.

"Helsinki 65-03-41?"

"This is 65-03-14. You must have misdialed."

"*Anteeksi*," the detective said, cursing himself under his breath. "Excuse me."

He replaced the receiver and redialed more slowly, repeating each number to himself as he did so. He heard the phone ring for several minutes before the decisive click as the line became live.

"Helsingin Kahvi," came a second female voice, more melodious than the previous one. Pitching somewhere near Middle C, it rose to a crescendo on the last syllable.

"I'm calling with regard to a Mr. John Ormond," he said. "I understand you may be holding something for him to collect." A direct approach like this, involving a degree of bluff, seemed to him the best option in limited circumstances.

"Your name, sir?" the woman enquired.

"George Mason, from London."

"Be kind to wait one moment."

He heard the receiver clatter onto a hard surface, followed by an indistinct muttering. At least, he thought, the line was still live.

"Good afternoon, Mr. Mason." It was a male voice this time, but with a strong native accent. "How can I assist you?"

"I am ringing on behalf of a Mr. John Ormond," the detective said, continuing his initial gambit. "I understand you may have something for him."

"There is nobody of that name here, sir. We employ only Finnish nationals."

"I know he doesn't work there," Mason said, testily. "Mr. Ormond is an English translator. He may have left some material to collect."

"We are coffee importers," the man replied. "Our business is exclusively with South America. We do occasionally use the services of a Spanish translator, a Senor Miguel Martinez based in Tampere, but no English."

"Sorry to trouble you in that case. Thanks for your time."

He replaced the receiver and began pacing the room again. It had been an outside chance at best, he told himself; but at least it was worth a try. The numbers must refer to *something*. Helvi Kilpinen should be home by now, he considered. As the person best acquainted with Ormond's habits and routine, the puzzling number-sequence might have some significance for her. Failing that, he could approach Forsenius. The police would have cryptic experts, decoders and the like, who might provide some useful pointers. Numbers had such a range of possibilities.

When Mason rang, Helvi was on the point of leaving her apartment to book theater tickets. It dashed his hopes that they might spend the evening together, over dinner perhaps in one of the more gourmet restaurants, instead of his continually relying on self-service establishments. She agreed to stop off at The Three Counts for a brief meeting, it being just across the street from the Swedish Theater. Mason hurriedly donned overcoat and hat, left the hotel and covered as briskly as he could over the impacted snow on the sidewalk the short distance along Mannerheim. The last thing he needed to do was to slip and injure himself. He reached the restaurant foyer ahead of her, brushed the light snow off his overcoat and waited several minutes before observing her leave the booking office opposite and, dodging the trams, stride breathlessly indoors to join him. With a tray of coffees, they were soon seated at their customary window table, looking down on the wintry scene.

"You still have no news of John?" she enquired, anxiously.

Mason shook his head, avoiding any mention of his trip to Siltasaari. It would only cause her alarm.

"This sort of enquiry takes time," he said. "We must be patient."

"But you are still hopeful, even though the Finnish police have given up?" There was a certain pleading look in her eyes which revealed how dependent she was on him.

He looked at her sympathetically.

"Major Forsenius told Uncle Paavo you thought there was little chance of finding him," she then challenged, with a hint of hostility in her tone. "He said you thought John had defected."

Mason cleared his throat and took a sip of the strong coffee. These coffee importers knew their stuff, he mused. This was top-quality Colombian.

"I must admit that the notion had crossed my mind," he said, "that he was involved with a Russian agent. But only because all the evidence seemed to point that way. In my business, one has to be realistic. It takes all sorts to make a society, and someone such as yourself, young and comparatively inexperienced in the ways of the world, if you will pardon me for saying so, might be more inclined to take people at face-value."

Helvi averted her eyes, unsure if that was a compliment or a criticism. They both fell silent for a few moments before she said, brightening:

"But now you are not so sure?"

"What Forsenius told your uncle—and I don't thank him for it—was never more than a working hypothesis. We must make the theories fit the facts, as far as possible."

"I think you were playing Devil's Advocate," she declared, a gleam of humor in her dark eyes.

The detective gazed ruefully back at her, that she could get so uncannily inside his mind.

"There may have been an element of that," he conceded, with a bland smile. "It's a quite legitimate technique."

"What makes you less certain now?"

"There are other parties active in this case."

His remark was greeted by a puzzled frown.

"The Russian Secret Service, in the shape of an agent known as the Lynx," he said, more specifically, "is taking a strong interest."

Helvi almost spilled her coffee.

"How could you possibly know that?" she asked, in amazement.

"I've been in contact with him."

"You don't say so!" she exclaimed, fearfully. "Did he mention John?"

"Not in so many words," he replied untruthfully, to spare her feelings. "But he may well know something. My guess is that he's more interested in recovering the manuscript."

"You mean *Zapiski Tarkov* is still here in Finland, after all this time?"

"It's beginning to look like that. And it may not be in Ormond's possession."

"Then he could not possibly have defected with it."

"In the sense that he disappeared with the manuscript, no," the detective was forced to concede.

Had it not been for the solid pine table between them, he sensed that Helvi might have hugged him there and then. Instead, she bestowed on him her most winning smile.

"It doesn't solve anything," he then said. "If anything, it makes things more complicated."

She grew thoughtful again. Uppermost in her mind was the still unanswered question: where was her English friend? She knew now that she could no longer ask him that. Hitherto, his various theorisings had provided some sort of explanation, which she had at least partially accepted as the truth. And with some degree of guarded optimism.

Aware that he had little time before she left, he reached inside his jacket pocket, withdrew the green ticket and placed it in front of her.

"Whatever is this?" she asked.

"It's a ticket for the Maly Theater in Leningrad. On the reverse is a number faintly written in pencil. I'm wondering if you might have any idea what it refers to."

Helvi took it and examined it with great interest.

"It's for a performance of the ballet *Flowers*," she said. "*Tsveti*, in Russian."

"But the number on the back? It's not a telephone number, I've already checked that out."

"Could be a lock combination, or a safe deposit number," the girl suggested.

Mason was impressed. "If you're right," he said, "it could mean that Ormond has placed the manuscript right here in Helsinki, somewhere under our very noses. Where would one find a safe depository?"

"A bank would be the most obvious place."

"That gives us a lot of options," Mason said. "There must be scores of banks in Helsinki. Do you happen to know where Ormond kept his account?"

"At the Bank of Karelia, on Mikonkatu. It's nearly opposite his place of work, the Polyglot Institute. I have been there several times with him, when he was depositing his pay-check."

"That's very helpful, Helvi," he remarked, gratefully. "I think we may well be onto something substantial at long last."

"Uncle Paavo will be extremely relieved if you can locate the manuscript. He blames himself for its disappearance."

"Why is this manuscript so important?" he asked.

"Because, so Unlce Paavo told me, it's a long way ahead of Russian official thinking. It promotes nuclear disarmament, democratic elections, green issues and a market economy."

"That's a whole bag of tricks," Mason declared, with feeling, "for an ideology committed to the death of capitalism."

"Exactly. Timor Tarkov urges the leadership to abandon ideological warfare and concentrate on matters nearer home, such as raising the standard of living for the average Russian."

"And if the West got hold of it?'

"It would be a tremendous psychological blow against the system," Helvi explained. "Since it would publicize abroad the extent of informed opposition inside Russia. Tarkov's status as a prominent academician lends great authority to his writings. Added to that, the underground dissident movement, through publication of the *samizdat*, is gaining momentum, making the leadership doubly sensitive to criticism. Uncle Paavo thinks great changes in Russian society are on the way, perhaps sooner rather than later."

"What you say is most interesting," Mason observed, "most interesting indeed. I had an entirely different impression of the book."

"How could you have *any* impression," the girl asked testily, "if you haven't read it?"

"Forsenius told me it was all about labor camps and secret prison hospitals."

"He must be confusing him with another author," Helvi remarked, obviously puzzled. "Solzhenitsin has written a lot about the gulags."

"Wouldn't surprise me," Mason said, thinking that the Finn, much like he himself, probably did not know *Das Kapital* from *Mein Kampf*. The world of intellectuals and their ideologies he treated with the distaste of the practical man. They were the ones who caused all the trouble in the first place, pitting one system against another, often with violent results. Ordinary people were the ones who suffered.

"And what are they playing at the Swedish Theater this evening?" he enquired, as his companion rose to leave.

"Ibsen's *Enemy of the People*," she replied. "Must hurry now, or I shall be late."

"Seems quite appropriate!" he quipped.

CHAPTER ELEVEN

FIRST THING THE following morning, George Mason called at the Bank of Karelia to find out if Helvi's hunch was correct. The moment he entered the Mikonkatu branch, he spied Arthur Greenwood and his secretary, Mrs Virtanen at the counter, hoping they had not spotted him. But the language school proprietor, having just deposited checks, turned and glanced his way.

"Inspector Mason!" he exclaimed.

The detective winced. "Morning!" he said simply, while crossing to the enquiry desk.

"Surprised to see you're still here," Greenwood said, "with only a few days left before Christmas. No news of our friend as yet, I suppose?"

"My enquiries are moving along quite nicely, given the circumstances."

"At the bank?" the other asked suspiciously, as if cottoning on to the fact that Mason's visit to the premises might have some connection with Ormond.

"Foreign currency," Mason replied matter-of-factly, to throw him off the scent. "Finnmarks, to be precise. Isn't that what they're called?"

Greenwood smiled knowingly, accepting the bluff. Mrs Virtanen, a pleasant, out-going woman, bade him a productive day and the two quickly left the bank.

"May I help you?" enquired the well-groomed, middle-aged woman at the enquiry desk.

"I wish to speak with the manager."

"Do you have an account here?"

The detective shook his head and, to avoid delay, produced official identity. The woman looked slightly perturbed and immediately put a call through to the manager's office. After a few moments a tall, balding individual dressed in an immaculate blue suit strode across the reception area to greet him.

"Mauno Rintala," he said genially, offering his hand. "Please step into my office."

Mason followed him into a thickly-carpeted area, tastefully furnished in mahogany, and accepted the offer of a seat in a deep-leather swivel-chair. It was a far cry from the relatively spartan accommodation at Police Headquarters.

"You're from Scotland Yard!" Rintala exclaimed in some astonishment, not without a strong hint of boyish enthusiasm.

Mason nodded. "I'm making some enquiries about an English translator who has gone missing from Helsinki. I understand he had an account at this branch."

"His name, Inspector?"

"John Ormond."

The manager turned towards his computer, keyed in an entry and waited for a few moments until the desired information showed up on the screen.

"His account's been dormant since the beginning of May."

"What is the last entry?" Mason wanted to know.

"A withdrawal, on April 30th."

"To clear his account?"

"By no means," Rintala said. "The remaining balance is substantial. He withdrew on that date two thousand Finnmarks."

Mason did a quick mental calculation. The sum withdrawn was roughly two hundred English pounds, enough perhaps for a week's expenses at most. It was beginning to look like Ormond had planned a short trip; much less like he had gone over to the other side. Even less likely was the remaining possibility, that he had been abducted, with or without the manuscript.

"It looks to me like he intended to take a short trip somewhere and failed to return. Where can one get to conveniently from here?"

"In the spring," Rintala replied, "weekend trips to Stockholm are very popular, on the overnight ferry."

"Anywhere else?"

"Estonia has only this year opened its borders to foreign tourists. Overnight ferry trips to Tallinn are being quite briskly booked. Went there with my wife Paivi in March."

"An interesting city, I believe?" the detective remarked.

"A quite beautifully preserved medieval city," the manager went on. "But not as modern and prosperous as Helsinki."

At that moment, George Mason would have bet a week's salary that that was precisely where John Ormond had gone. The amount he had withdrawn, considering hotel and meal outlays, would have sufficed for an extended weekend, hardly for a full week. He was in half a mind to go there himself and see if he could track Ormond down, except that Harrington wanted him to concentrate his main effort on recovering the manuscript.

"I expect you have a safe depository?" he then said.

"We certainly do," Rintala replied.

"Is it possible to ascertain if John Ormond made us of it?"

"You mean, has he placed something there for safe-keeping?"

The detective nodded.

"That would be a highly confidential matter, Inspector Mason. In any case we could not access it without a specific warrant from the city police."

"Let us first establish the fact," Mason argued. "Major Viljo Forsenius will issue any authorizations that may become necessary."

"Let me speak with my senior clerk," the manager said. "For security reasons, you will appreciate, such information does not show up on the computer."

In his absence, Mason mused on what a useful hunch it had been of Helvi Kilpinen's to try this line of enquiry. If Mauno Rintala returned with safe deposit number 650341, he had hit the jackpot. He would claim the manuscript, return to London with it and alert the Foreign Office about a certain English national presumed missing in Tallinn. It would become diplomatic, rather than police business. But the expression on the bank manager's face on re-entering his office told him quite clearly that he was out of luck.

"The senior clerk, Ahti Savonen," Rintala explained, "claims that Mr. Ormond has never used our safe-depository. He has checked all the records thoroughly."

Mason eased his portly frame out of the comfortable chair and shook the manager's hand.

"Thanks very much for your help," he said, on leaving. "I really appreciate it."

"Not at all," the genial manager said. "Only too pleased to assist a representative of Scotland Yard. Conan Doyle and Agatha Christie are among our favorite authors."

"If Ormond's account reactivates," Mason said, recalling a similar, more caustic, remark of Forsenius's, "please let me know at once."

"With due police authorization, certainly," Rintala agreed.

*

On leaving the bank, he turned left along Mikonkatu until he reached Esplanade, from where it was a short walk to South

Harbor. A small crowd had gathered at the dockside. Here, where everything was so calm and uneventful round the ice-locked bay, a kind of living hibernation, the slightest untoward event was sufficient to arouse the interest of passers-by. Turning up his coat collar and adjusting the ear-muffs which were the latest addition to his winter apparel, he crossed the market square to join them. The dockside engine had jammed in the frozen points and the large mobile crane had moved into place in an attempt to lift it. The stevedores' breath rose in a freezing vapor above their heads as they labored in the sub-zero morning air with a minimum of fuss and a touch of typically Finnish wry humor. Anticipating that the difficult operation would take all morning at least, he left the small group of onlookers and soon gained the interior of Police Headquarters.

Major Forsenius, accustomed by now to the detective dropping by at any odd time during the day, put the finishing touches to a report he was compiling before glancing up to acknowledge his presence. The desk telephone rang at the same moment and, while the major answered it, Mason crossed to the office window to see how the engineering operation was getting on. The rear end of the locomotive had now been raised well above the track, sparks lit up the somber sky and the same pall of freezing breath hovered above workmen and onlookers alike. He would hate to see a mainline express derailed in conditions like this. It would take days to rectify.

"Something wrong out there?" Forsenius eventually asked, without rising from his chair.

"The dockside engine ran foul of the points," Mason said. "I expect it happens fairly often at this time of year."

"They're always having problems. The track needs relaying in places. Something the Russians built pre-1917. But you haven't come to discuss the finer points of stevedoring?"

The detective turned from the window and smiled. Perhaps he knew more than the Finn suspected, from the few years he had spent in London's dockland. A job with Alsatian dogs, patrolling the riverside at night.

"Thought I'd bring you up-to-date on recent developments," he said. "That is, if you're not too occupied."

"Just completing paper work," Forsenius said, genially. "What's new?"

"The other side have again shown their hand."

"Another tip-off about Siltasaari?" he quipped.

"That's most likely a red herring, designed to throw us off the scent. I strongly suspect that John Ormond left Helsinki on April 30th, quite possibly for Tallinn. He withdrew two thousand Finnmarks from his bank account on that day, enough for a long weekend. Had he gone to Stockholm, or even Copenhagen, he would presumably have returned long since. Whether he reached his destination, or remained subsequently in Estonia, is another question entirely."

"You called at his bank?" the Finn asked, much impressed.

Mason pulled out the Maly Theater ticket and passed it across the desk.

"I thought the number scribbled on the back might refer to a safe-deposit. Helvi Kilpinen told me where he kept his account."

The Finn raised skeptical eyebrows as he examined it.

"Could refer to anything," he said. "I'll have our cryptographers look at it to see if they can come up with some ideas. It may, for example, be some sort of code, the digits standing for letters of the alphabet. It may even prove entirely innocent. A lottery ticket number, perhaps."

"Or it may mean nothing at all," the detective had to admit.

"Just doodling?" asked the other, with a humorous glint in his eye.

"An odd sort of doodle though, don't you think?"

The major placed the green ticket beneath his desk blotter, wrote a memorandum on his note-pad, and said:

"What about our friend, Maxim Ivanovich? Has he resurfaced recently?"

"Yesterday, while I was out, someone gained entry to my hotel room and went through all my belongings. I assume it was the same party that sent us on a wild goose chase to Kotka."

"What do you imagine they were looking for?" Forsenius asked, rising from his chair in concern.

"Some clue, no doubt, as to the whereabouts of *The Tarkov Papers*."

"That means they think you've got your nose in front. Otherwise, they would hardly risk a daylight raid. Why did you not report this incident immediately to us?"

"Nothing appeared to be missing," Mason said. "Whatever they were after, they did not find it. There was nothing to find, apart perhaps from that green ticket, which I always kept in my pocket, inside the diary."

"So you have no other concrete leads?"

"I suspect Arthur Greenwood knows a lot more than he is letting on."

"What makes you say that?"

"It was through him that Ormond met Maxim. The translation of the program for the Vladimir Dance Ensemble was handled by the Polyglot Institute, via the Russian Embassy. It would be the last piece of translation Ormond worked on. Greenwood wouldn't say outright that the two met, nor does he admit to knowing Maxim himself."

"Deep water for a language school," Forsenius observed. "Aren't you reading too much into this?"

"Greenwood's agency has well-established contacts with the embassy. They handle all their English translation needs."

"That doesn't mean they run a spy-ring on the side. Translation is a very legitimate business."

"Even when a top Russian agent is involved?"

The major crossed to the window and gazed out pensively across the bay.

"They managed to fix the light engine," he remarked, casually. "It's up and running in fine style for a vintage locomotive."

"Good to see a steam engine in operation," the detective agreed. "They've been largely superannuated in Britain, apart from summer tourist runs."

Forsenius turned away from the dockside scene and resumed his seat behind a large, cluttered desk that spoke of volumes of police work even in law-abiding Finland.

"What you should bear in mind, Inspector," he said, after a thoughtful pause, "is that half the embassy staff are agents of one sort or another, be it political, economic, military or industrial espionage. Where do you draw the line? In any case, if Greenwood is involved, he will have his traces well-covered by now. What could we possibly charge him with?"

"That might depend on whether or not John Ormond resurfaces. Couldn't you at least revoke his residence permit?"

"That would mean closing down his language school," the Finn said, doubtfully. "One that provides a very useful service, both culturally and commercially, to the inhabitants of this city. My wife Soili took lessons there not so very long ago. Of course, if your suspicions about him are substantiated, we shall then have to take a fresh look at the permit question."

"And ship him back to England as an undesirable alien? Harrington will have a field day."

"Harrington?" the other queried.

"The head of Special Branch."

"Sitting comfortably behind a desk at Scotland Yard?" he jibed.

"Right now," Mason said, glancing at his watch, "he'll be having the first tot of his favorite single malt, along with his morning coffee."

"Glenmorangie?" enquired the knowledgeable Finn.

"Glenfiddich, as a matter of fact."

"Your alcohol laws are far less restrictive than ours, perhaps because you handle it better. But more to the point, we'll have our experts look at this number sequence here and see what they come up with. Scribbled on a Leningrad theater ticket, it may be a local phone number there, or something similar. I wouldn't hold out too much hope. I'll get in touch as soon as I can. Meanwhile, good hunting!"

George Mason had the uneasy sensation of being followed on the way back to his hotel after taking leave of Forsenius, and again as he made his way after a quick lunch to Hotel Kivi. He recognized with some amusement that he was beginning to acquire native habits, much preferring the sauna bath for his ritual cleansing than the cramped shower in his hotel room. For one thing, it was more sociable, to sit there sweating it out with the hardy types who were regular clients, and afterwards to be scrubbed by the no-nonsense *saunatajat*. One emerged far cleaner, more relaxed and more invigorated, perhaps even a little wiser, from the rigorous procedure. As he took his place in the hot room, careful to douse a piece of board under the cold tap to sit on to avoid scalding his haunches, his initial reaction was that Major Forsenius, concerned for his safety, had set one of his officers to shadow his movements.

Since he could not be sure Forsenius was behind it, he resolved to take extra precautions when he set out that same evening for his dinner engagement at the Kilpinens, partly to avoid placing his hosts in any danger. On leaving his hotel, he made his way on foot along Mannerheim to the tram stop by the Swedish Theater. He knew by now that many of the city's tram routes were circular. The Number 3 would take him within a few minutes to the Brunnspark, where the Kilpinens lived; or he could take it in the opposite direction and arrive at the same destination forty-five minutes later. He had allowed himself time to effect this little ruse, on the assumption he had been followed from the hotel.

He did not wait very long for a tram. As the doors of the ultra-modern vehicle closed silently behind him and the driver suddenly accelerated to catch a green light, he noticed out of the corner of his eye a dark figure step back quickly into the shadow of the theater, on the Esplanade side, away from the well-lit foyer. It was too brief a glimpse to ascertain whether or not the man wore a beard, in a city of clean-shaven men. But it was enough to confirm his misgivings that his movements were now being closely watched; that they were, incredible as it seemed to him at that moment, entering the end-game in this whole mysterious business. Was he, he wondered, as the major had suggested, one step ahead of the opposition? It was almost beginning to look that way, even in the absence of hard facts to support that view.

Having made the lights, the tram picked up speed past Linnanmaki Amusement Park, closed down for the winter, and the equally deserted Olympic Stadium, whose modern lines stood out starkly against the night sky. Mason relaxed into his seat, prepared for the longish ride until the tram came almost full circle to the harbor. A brisk walk across Brunnspark would then bring him to the diplomatic quarter and the Kilpinens' apartment. The dark rows of tenements which they passed were relieved only by the brightly-lit foyers of small cinemas, still the most popular form of entertainment in the Finnish capital. James Bond or Eddie Constantine stared down at him from a succession of illuminated hoardings. If only real-life detective work were as glamorous as that! George Mason with his name in lights, instead of combing the snow-clad streets dodging shadows.

In due course the tram came to a halt outside the terminal for the Stockholm ferry. The building was in semi-darkness until passengers began to arrive for the overnight passage and Mason was a little slow in recognizing it as his stop. Jumping from his seat, he managed to jam his foot in the closing doors, causing them to spring back open with a loud clatter. The conductor gave him a stern look of disapproval as he caught his breath in the raw night air and placed uncertain footsteps on the crisp snow-surface. The vehicle sped off, leaving him in almost total darkness, the frozen bay on the one hand, the dark void of the city's main park yawning before him on the other. It proved easier to traverse than he had anticipated. Fresh ski-tracks criss-crossed the area, weaving in and out of the clumps of pines. He found he could make good progress placing his feet in them, at the same time conscious of how exposed he was in the event of someone wishing him harm. The shadowy figure by the Swedish Theater came to mind. He surely would not still be standing there and he wondered uneasily, fully aware how resourceful the opposition was, if that individual had somehow anticipated his itinerary. It was with considerable relief that, after foot-slogging through the snow, he espied the lighted windows of the residential apartments. He made sure no one was lurking in the vicinity of the Kilpinen residence before entering and ringing the doorbell.

Helvi answered his summons, greeting him with a welcoming smile.

"Good evening. Inspector Mason," she said. "Have trouble locating us?"

"Came the long way round," he replied, without explaining why, as the warm glow of the apartment interior flowed past her out onto the landing. "Apologies for keeping you waiting."

She hung up his coat, hat and ear-muffs in the small vestibule and led him through to the living-room, with its highly-polished parquet floor, designer rugs, contemporary furniture and aromas of cooking-in-progress from the adjacent kitchen. Uncle Paavo rose from his seat in a window alcove to greet him.

"Major Forsenius tells me you may have some more definite leads at last," he said, a ray of hope dawning across his strained features.

"Nothing too conclusive," the detective admitted, guardedly.

"Please take a seat, Inspector," Paavo said, with a look poised between anticipation and disappointment. "Can I offer you a drink?"

"Scotch and soda, please."

"Single malt? I have the Glenlivet."

"That will do very nicely," Mason said, reminded strongly of Harrington's predilections.

"The major seemed quite up-beat when I spoke to him this morning," the host then said.

"Major Forsenius knows even less than I do. However, the picture isn't quite so bleak as it was a week ago."

Paavo's expression relaxed to a half-smile and they made small talk, about malt whisky and the severe weather, while Helvi busied herself in the kitchen.

"Do you have plans for Christmas?" Paavo eventually asked.

The question took the detective by surprise.

"I was hoping to spend it in London, with my wife Adele. That is, if we can get this business cleared up."

"If you're marooned here, Helvi and I would be most pleased to have you for dinner."

Mason felt genuinely touched by such spontaneous generosity. Nothing would please him more in the circumstances.

"That's very kind of you," he said. "I should be happy to accept your invitation."

"Then that's settled."

They transferred to the dining table as Helvi served a light meal of his favorite reindeer steak, wild rice and asparagus tips. Paavo uncorked a bottle of Mosel.

"Last year," Paavo remarked, "John Ormond joined us for Christmas dinner."

"Poor chap," Mason said. "I wonder where he'll be spending this Christmas."

"You know, he was a very likeable sort of person, with a typical English diffidence and a dry sense of humor. There is something in the English character very similar to the Finnish temperament. I suppose that's why we took to him so readily."

"You are talking about him in the past tense," Mason observed.

Paavo looked a little embarrassed.

"Whatever has befallen him, Inspector, I am only too aware that it is I, more than anyone else, who is responsible."

"Excellent Riesling," Mason said, in an attempt to de-fuse the tension.

"Come, uncle," Helvi interjected. "Don't blame yourself. Both of you realized the implications of undertaking such a task."

"I certainly did," her uncle replied. "Whether John did or not, I am not so sure."

"What exactly do you mean?" Mason asked.

"To him, it was an exciting challenge. He was so keen to do literary translation, as a step up from commercial and legal texts, I doubt he had weighed the political implications. Or the risks involved."

"Surely," Mason interposed, "he appreciated the full significance of the manuscript. Otherwise, he would not have taken steps to conceal it."

The remark had an electric effect on Paavo Kilpinen.

"You say he *hid* the manuscript?" he asked, in bewilderment.

The detective nodded.

"How could you possibly know that?"

"The KGB are still very active in this matter. If they are holding Ormond, they cannot also have the manuscript. My assumption is that he left it somewhere for safe-keeping, before he disappeared. Thought you might have some ideas."

"He certainly did not leave it with me," Paavo hastened to make clear. "What about his employer?"

"Arthur Greenwood maintains complete ignorance of the whole business, whether genuinely or not I am not so sure."

"Did you try the bank depository?" Helvi asked, encouragingly.

"Drew a blank," the detective said, savoring the crisp dryness of the Mosel. "Tell me, Helvi, did Ormond mention anything to you about taking a trip abroad at the end of April?"

"Why do you ask that?" she asked, with puzzled concern.

"Because he withdrew two thousand Finnmarks from his bank account about that time."

"I find that very odd," Helvi said. "I'm sure he would have mentioned it to me. He has always in the past told me about his trips."

"For example?"

"Last year, he flew to New England for an autumn foliage tour. Leaf-peeping, he called it."

"I suspect he went to Tallinn," Mason announced. "But I have no definite proof."

"Tallinn?" both Kilpinens cried, simultaneously.

"That's what I figure," Mason said. It was as if he had dropped a bombshell.

"Then it must have been a spur-of-the-moment decision," Helvi said, when the information had finally sunk in, "in reaction to some sudden turn of events."

"Quite possibly," Mason agreed. "But why has he not returned?"

The trio completed their appetizing meal in silence. Uncle Paavo topped up their wine glasses, then crossed to the window to lower the venetian blind.

"By the way, Inspector," he remarked, "you did come alone, didn't you?"

The detective's fork remained poised between his plate and his lips, as an uneasy thought crossed his mind and he felt his stomach muscles begin to tighten.

"What exactly do you mean?" he asked.

"It's probably nothing, Inspector. Just now I noticed someone standing in the street below. He seemed to glance up at our window."

Mason placed the forkful of steak in his mouth and chewed it slowly, saying nothing.

"You've gone very quiet," Helvi said. "Is something the matter?"

"Is there a rear entrance to this building?" he suddenly asked.

Paavo and Helvi exchanged wary looks.

"There's a service entrance on the ground floor," Paavo said. "I'll take you that way when you leave, if you're concerned."

"Could be something or nothing in this game of shadows. I doubt in any case he will remain there very long. It must be well below zero."

Both Kilpinens smiled at his remark. The evening was still comparatively young and there were many things to talk about.

"Cloudberries, with frozen yoghurt for dessert," Helvi said, to lighten the atmosphere.

"Cloudberries?" their puzzled visitor asked.

"Picked from the forest swamps up north," she replied. "They're considered a great delicacy."

While she went briefly to the kitchen, Paavo returned to the subject of the missing manuscript.

"Timor Tarkov rang me the other day," he said. "From Geneva. He had no idea Ormond had gone missing and his manuscript along with him. He nearly went ballistic. I mentioned that Scotland Yard and the Helsinki police were working flat-out to recover it. But I did not say anything about Maxim. He's going to ring me every few days, for news of developments."

"I thought you might have some idea where Ormond could have hidden it," Mason said. "From your knowledge of his work routines."

"I assume he did his translation work mostly at home," Paavo replied. "Have you checked his Kulosaari apartment?"

"The very first place I visited. I wasn't seeking a missing manuscript at that point, however. The place had already been thoroughly gone through. All I recovered of use was his diary."

Helvi returned from the kitchen to serve the dessert. Of the trio, she seemed the most relaxed. Young as she was, she displayed an intuitive feminine skepticism of male intrigue, and her composure acted like a balm on the nerves of her more anxious uncle. The detective noted with interest the differences in their demeanor.

"They look like large raspberries," he remarked of the appetizing dessert. "Except for their pale-yellow color. Quite delicious."

"Glad you like them," the girl said, with evident pleasure.

"A cognac with your coffee?" his host offered, rising to cross to the cabinet by the window.

"Don't mind if I do," his guest replied, persuading himself that he was not really drinking on duty. It was more like an evening off.

Glancing for a moment through the slats of the venetian blind, Paavo said:

"All clear down below. Don't see a living thing."

"I expect it was just one of Forsenius's men keeping an eye on me," Mason said, to put them at ease. "Probably signed off and gone home. All the same, I may use the rear door when I leave, if you don't mind."

Paavo and Helvi exchanged significant looks, but did not press the point.

"I was wondering," the detective said, nursing his brandy, "where would be the likeliest place to conceal a book manuscript?"

"Are you really so much in the dark, after all this time?" Paavo asked, pointedly.

"The Inspector is speaking hypothetically," Helvi countered. "He's not going to tell us everything he knows. He simply wants our ideas, our input."

George Mason could have hugged her at that point, and might have done had the table not stood between them, so supportive of him did she seem.

"The likeliest place to hide a manuscript?" a half-inebriated Paavo mused aloud.

Mason chased the coffee with the cognac, curious in an amused sort of way as to what his host might come up with. Helvi looked on, expectantly.

"Tell me, Inspector," the other said, after a few moments, "if you wished to hide an apple, where would you put it?"

Was he hearing correctly, Mason wondered? Was this some sort of traditional folk wisdom of the Finns, or was Uncle Paavo pulling his leg?

"Why, in a barrel of apples, of course."

Paavo smiled in triumph, but the detective only frowned. He did not care for riddles. His was one of those practical minds that proceeded step by step to a logical conclusion, rather than relying on sudden flashes of insight. Those could safely be left to the rising generation of graduates in criminology who were increasingly entering the service.

"You are not following my train of thought," Paavo said.

"I agree," Mason conceded, "that the best place to conceal an apple would be in a barrel of apples; or a banana on a banana boat, for that matter. But you are surely not suggesting that Ormond left *The Tarkov Papers* among his other books? It would have been discovered long ago."

"Not in his own small library," the other theorized. "Perhaps in a public library."

A slow smile spread across the detective's chubby features.

"You may just have a point there," he admitted. "But surely there are many public libraries in Helsinki."

"John quite often used the University Reference Library," Helvi remarked. "It's not very far from the Polyglot Institute."

"Such places are in constant use by the general public," Mason said. "Anyone could have walked off with it."

"Perhaps he meant for it to be discovered," Helvi suggested, "so that it would not fall into the wrong hands."

"That's also a possibility," the detective agreed, thinking it significant that the translator did not in that event mention the fact to Arthur Greenwood.

"The University Library contains tens of thousands of books," Paavo remarked. "You'd have your work cut out to go through them all."

Mason groaned inwardly. Was he ever going to get to the bottom of all this? The plot seemed to thicken at every turn. Did John Ormond travel to Tallinn, or did he not? Was the manuscript still in Helsinki, or was it not? Was Forsenius shadowing him, or was it Maxim?

The evening wore on, almost imperceptibly. The Kilpinens plied him with more food and drink and the conversation eventually turned on more general themes, on Finnish music, literature and the plastic arts. Uncle Paavo got around to showing him various objets d'art he had collected from different parts of the globe, particularly from Africa, the stock-in-trade of his antiques business. As the hands of the clock moved towards eleven, he rose rather unsteadily to his feet to take his leave, with the feeling that it had been very a satisfying, if still inconclusive, evening. He thanked them warmly for their hospitality.

"Rather than have you leave by the rear entrance, I'll call you a cab," Uncle Paavo offered. "It's a bit late to catch a tram. They stop running at eleven."

CHAPTER TWELVE

G EORGE MASON SLEPT late the following morning, from the effects of the Kilpinens' hospitality. It was almost nine o'clock when he roused himself sufficiently to call room service. While waiting, he took a quick shower, dressed and crossed to the window to peer between the slats of the venetian blind to make sure no one was watching from the doorways in the street below, recalling with some misgivings the unexplained presence outside the Kilpinen apartment. The street was quiet. There were few pedestrians about by this hour, most having disappeared into the well-heated offices and shops of the city center. A rap on his door announced the arrival of morning coffee. Accepting the small tray from the attractive young waitress, he placed it on his bedside table, then checked the date on his calendar. It was December 21st, the winter solstice. Small wonder it was still barely daylight in the Finnish capital; it would be dark again by three o'clock.

He had barely commenced his light refreshment when the telephone rang.

"Good morning, Inspector Mason," came the brisk voice of Viljo Forsenius, whom the detective estimated would have been at his desk for at least an hour. "Did you sleep well?"

"Excellently," Mason replied, feeling he had rarely slept better.

"Our experts have been examining your, or rather Ormond's, green theater ticket. An interesting item, certainly. But the number sequence is neither a Leningrad nor a Tallinn phone number; nor is it a lottery number, bank account or social security number."

"That seems to cover all the options," Mason said, feeling disappointed.

"Something you may have missed yourself, however, is a decimal point so faint that it only shows up under magnification. The number on the back actually reads: 650.341."

Mason jotted it down on hotel notepaper, exactly as the major read it.

"I was thinking of coming round later this morning," he said, "if that's convenient?"

"Actually not," Forsenius said. "There's a police conference all morning. I'm just on the point of leaving. Thought I'd bring you up-to-date."

"Until later then," the detective said, ringing off.

It was only as he sat down again on the edge of the bed to finish his coffee that the force of what the major had said hit him. He got up and paced the room excitedly. Paavo's homespun wisdom about barrels of apples might just, incredibly, be correct. What Forsenius had just read out to him, he realized, was the Dewey Classification System for library books. Tarkov's script was at this very moment probably gathering dust on a shelf of the University Reference Library, or his name was not George Mason. He laughed out loud. Christmas in London with Adele and their skiing trip to the Dolomites loomed large in his mind, almost crowding out everything else.

As his sense of elation gradually subsided, he began to think of practicalities. Right now, he considered, he was not one, but at least two large steps ahead of the opposition. Not in a hundred years would Maxim Ivanovich, alias the Lynx, and his associates at the KGB tumble to the whereabouts of the missing manuscript. The laugh was definitely on them. Slipping on his overcoat, fur hat and ear-muffs to face the wintry day, he went downstairs and was barely past reception when the desk clerk called him back.

"A gentleman called," the clerk said. "A few minutes ago. He asked if you had already left the hotel."

Mason froze in his tracks, feeling his stomach muscles tighten and his pulse start to race.

"A gentleman with a beard?" he asked, guardedly.

The clerk shook his head.

"And what did you tell him?"

"I told him I thought you were still resting."

"In future," Mason said, "say nothing. I want no visitors of any description."

It occurred to him to check with Forsenius in case the major was shadowing him for his own safety. But the Finn would already have left for his conference. The alternative, that it was one of Maxim's men, was more disturbing in that it implied they were now moving more into the open, beyond the cryptic calls over the love-lines at the Havis Club and red herrings to Siltasaari.

Curious, he thought as he left the hotel, that such a move should coincide with his key break-through in the case. The opposition were evidently kept well-informed and he began to wonder who, in this city of frequently ambiguous loyalties, was keeping them abreast of events. Arthur Greenwood came to mind, but he dismissed the idea. The language school proprietor was not well-versed in the latest stages of the game. Paavo and Helvi Kilpinen were palpably genuine and loyal, and Viljo Forsenius was someone he *had* to trust one hundred per cent.

Snow was falling quite heavily as he directed his steps towards the university, down near South Harbor and not very far from Police Headquarters, so that he did not hear the steps of the person trying to catch up with him before the man was already abreast. Mason stopped in his tracks and turned, to be confronted by a short, dapper, very respectable-looking gentleman.

"Excuse me, Mr. Mason," the man said. "Allow me to introduce myself. My name is Andreas Lovinas, of the Latvian Trade Delegation. I tried to catch you earlier at your hotel."

The detective felt the tension flow out of him, his main reaction being one of surprise.

"Is there somewhere we can talk, out of this hard weather?"

Mason was hesitant. He had urgent business to attend to.

"It will only take a few minutes of your time," Lovinas said. "It's a matter of crucial importance to my delegation."

Something about his manner, and his general air of respectability, prevailed upon the detective, who was also aware that Latvia was next door to Estonia. The man might just know something of the missing translator. They were almost level with a French pastry shop called *La Baguette*, whose aroma of French roast lingered temptingly round the entrance.

"A quick coffee then," Mason said, leading the way inside.

Once seated, Andreas Lovinas adopted a friendly, one might almost say, confidential attitude.

"How did you know my name?" Mason asked, sharply.

Lovinas smiled. "Helsinki is a small city," he remarked, disarmingly. "It is difficult to preserve one's anonymity for very long."

You bet, was Mason's unspoken reaction, sensing that the next topic of their conversation would be the missing manuscript.

"It has come to our attention," the other said, "that you may have information concerning the whereabouts of a certain literary property which went astray in this country some months ago."

The detective merely returned a neutral stare, saying nothing. Lovinas was not deterred.

"Our delegation is willing to offer a considerable sum for it," he said. "Many times your annual salary."

"You've done research on that?" Mason asked, not entirely surprised.

"We have an efficient economics section. 'Comparative statistics on the pay of European public servants'. Quite elementary material, I assure you."

The detective sipped his coffee in some bemusement. Bribery was about the last gambit he expected from the other side, who were evidently completely at sea. When the soft-sell in the person of this professional diplomat failed, he had no doubt they would bring in the heavies.

"What language do they speak in Latvia?" he asked, changing the subject.

"Lettish," replied Lovinas.

"Do you happen to know anything of the whereabouts of an English translator who may have left Helsinki for Tallinn at the end of April last?"

Lovinas's eyes narrowed. "Many people visit Estonia now, since they opened their borders to visa-free tourism."

"His name was John Ormond."

"I know no one of that name," the other declared. He waited for a few moments before saying: "Are you willing to consider our offer?"

"I have no idea what you are referring to," Mason replied, pointedly.

"I think you know very well what I am referring to," Lovinas said, coldly. "One hundred thousand Finnmarks is a very generous offer."

It would almost buy me a new car, Mason mused, intrigued at how desperate the other side must be.

"If I knew what you meant by 'literary property'," he replied, "your offer might make some sense."

"I can see that you are not open to negotiate," the other said, quickly draining his coffee. "I hope for your sake that you will not regret it."

"Is that a threat or a promise?" the detective asked.

"Take it any way you like," Lovinas said, scowling from the doorway.

When he had gone, Mason fell to wondering how much they really knew and how much was pure bluff. One thing was clear. They were very determined to recover *The Tarkov Papers* and would stop at nothing. He was beginning to feel he may require the assistance of Forsenius at a critical moment and that it would be prudent to wait until the major's morning conference was over. He paid for both coffees and retraced his steps to the main station concourse, to kill time browsing through the boutiques for last-minute presents.

It was nearly midday when he caught the Number 3 tram outside the main station, having taken the opportunity for an overdue hair-trim at the busy barber's shop opposite the platform where the secretive Leningrad express was stationed, ahead of its evening departure. The strains of *Silent Night*, in its hauntingly beautiful Finnish rendering, were clearly audible from Station Square, striking an odd note of discord with his present mood. The city was doggedly going about its normal business in the run-up to the festive season. What did Christmas mean, he mused, to the likes of Maxim Ivanovich and Andreas Lovinas, members of societies whose official creed was atheistic materialism? He was aware then, as the tram moved silently away, that two men, quite likely the strong arm of the Estonian Trade Delegation, had followed him aboard, sitting stonily together at the rear of the carriage.

Mason was not unduly concerned, since he doubted that they would be bold enough actually to follow him inside the University Reference Library. They were as much in the dark as Lovinas and could hardly make a move before their quarry was firmly in sight. The tram proceeded slowly, impeded by the build-up of traffic heading towards the harbor. When it finally reached the university precinct, Mason alighted and began climbing the long flight of stone steps towards the main entrance, past young, fur-clad students conversing in small groups despite the cold. As he had surmised, the two men did not follow him up. He caught their reflection in the glass of the revolving doors, saw them hovering at the base of the steps and light cigarettes before one of them strode towards the telephone kiosk. Within minutes, no doubt, either Lovinas or Maxim, perhaps both together, would appear and invest the scene with fresh authority. It would then be four against one.

The presence just inside the revolving doors of a uniformed commissionaire checking bags and briefcases reassured him. Probably ex-army, the detective thought; someone who would know how to react to a crisis. Behind him, a young brunette was seated at a long counter sorting what appeared to be readers' cards. A second, older woman a few feet away was working at a computer. It being the end of the autumn term, only a handful of students were poring over their books in the large reading-room to the left.

"*Huomenta,*" the young librarian said, glancing up. "Good morning."

Mason returned the greeting in his best Finnish, at the same time glancing over his shoulder to make doubly sure he had not been followed. That put the girl slightly on her guard.

"Are you a member here?" she asked.

"Er . . . no," he replied, cagily. "I merely wish to consult the main reference section for a few minutes."

"Are you a journalist?" she asked, feeling the need for her own peace of mind to categorize him.

"Just personal research," he said, passing the green theater ticket across the counter, so that she could read the number.

"Since most of our students have already gone down for the holidays," she said, "I see no harm in that."

She swiveled round to the card index beside her, while Mason held his breath. To draw a blank here would mean the end of everything. He would withdraw from the case as defeated as Maxim.

"650 is encyclopedias," she explained. "Through the right-hand arch, then take the second door on your left." She waved a heavily-ringed right hand in the general direction and returned to her task.

Mason thanked her and set off to explore the library, relieved that she had allowed him, a complete outsider, to use restricted student facilities. Where else would that be possible, he mused, except in a country like Finland, which set such high store on education and freedom of information? Small wonder it had just about the highest rate of literacy in the world.

Her directions led him to a quiet room at the rear of the building, where tall shelves of bound volumes rose almost to the ceiling. The classification sequence began at 650.100. His eye traveled upwards and across, until he spotted on the topmost shelf the reference 650.300. Ascending the librarians' ladder, he soon found himself examining the faded blue bindings of older editions of ENCYCLOPEDIA FENNICA. They had gathered dust from years, possibly decades, of disuse.

After a brief search, the number 650.341 stared back at him with an almost magical quality. It classified the 1965 edition of the bulky reference work. He removed it carefully and placed it on the ladder shelf, thinking that this would be the ideal place to conceal a manuscript in the confident expectation that it would not be discovered or disturbed. Behind the volumes he discerned a large Manila envelope secured by a stout elastic band. He nearly fell from the ladder in his eagerness. Grasping it gingerly, as if it contained hundred-mark bills, he withdrew it from its hiding-place and read the title in large Cyrillic capitals: ZAPISKI TARKOV. His feelings of excitement, vindication and triumph were tempered only by the very real practical problem of how to get it safely past the opposition. Descending the ladder with his trophy, he checked his watch. At least Forsenius, who would be blown over by his discovery, should by now be free of his morning duties and Police Headquarters were only a few blocks away.

There was only one way now that he could leave the library unscathed, he considered, as he strode purposefully up to the young brunette sitting at the counter.

"Call the police immediately," he rapped. "A burglary is about to take place."

The girl stared back at him in alarm, but complied at once.

"Ask for Major Forsenius," he insisted.

"Do you wish to speak to him yourself?"

Mason nodded curtly, placing the bulky Manila package on the counter in front of her. She looked at it uncertainly, not recognizing it as library property, before handing him the telephone receiver.

"Inspector Mason," came the faintly ironic voice of the Finn. "What the Dickens are you doing at the university?"

"I'll reveal all as soon as you arrive. Just get here on the double, and bring reinforcements."

"Give me ten minutes," Forsenius said, with a half-audible curse. "And don't do anything rash. The last thing we want is an international incident."

Mason handed the receiver back to the librarian, who now looked as puzzled as she was alarmed at the prospect of the police invading the quiet precincts of the library.

"Would it be too much to ask what all this is about?" she said. "I don't see any sign of burglars, yet you have called the police. Are you by any chance concealing library documents in this envelope?"

"Not strictly speaking," he replied, airily. "But you can examine for yourself the contents of this package, if you wish."

The girl pondered the offer for a moment, but declined and returned to sorting cards. At that moment, Mason noticed the two gentlemen from the tram approaching the top of the long flight of steps. Concealing the Manila envelope beneath his topcoat, he reached the revolving doors just as they were entering, catching them off-guard and bundling them inside the building as he made his way as quickly as he could down the steps. He had reached half-way when his progress was arrested by a rasping voice just ahead of him.

"Not so fast, Inspector Mason. A fall on this ice could result in serious injury."

Mason stopped in his tracks. To his chagrin, found himself peering into a broad, bearded face beneath a black Pushkin hat, at the same time noticing two back-up agents closing in on them from the square below.

"You could have saved yourself a lot of trouble, Inspector," Maxim said, "by co-operating with Mr. Lovinas, of the Estonian Trade Delegation, when you left your hotel."

Mason quickly weighed the odds, feeling instinctively for the Beretta Forsenius had lately insisted that he carry.

"I wouldn't draw a weapon, Inspector, if I were you. My men are expert marksmen."

The detective let both arms drop to his sides, aware that the envelope was protruding slightly from beneath his coat. Maxim's eyes fixed on it in triumph.

"My congratulations, too, are in order," the Russian said, expansively. "Your detective work was first-rate. We were pretty sure you would lead us to *Zapiski Tarkov* sooner or later. Now that you have fulfilled our expectations, please hand over the manuscript."

As he spoke, there was a screech of car brakes in the square below. It was now Maxim's turn to weigh the odds as police personnel from three squad cars, led by Major Viljo Forsenius, swiftly alighted and ascended the steps. The expression on the Russian's face changed abruptly from one of triumph to one of mortified defeat. The sporadic groups of students observed intently the dramatic scene, as eight Helsinki police now surrounded the five Russians, including the two who had re-appeared from the library.

"Your move, Maxim Ivanovich," Mason said, as if they were playing chess.

"Checkmate, it seems to me," Forsenius said pointedly, relieving Mason of the Manila package under the covetous eyes of the Russian.

Maxim made a stiff, formal bow in acknowledgment of defeat.

"You even discovered my identity, Inspector Mason," he said, with grudging admiration. "When all along I considered my cover near-perfect."

"The Vladimir Dance Ensemble?" Mason replied. "Wish I had seen the show."

"If you would now accompany us to Police Headquarters," Forsenius said, "we shall have some questions to put to you regarding the disappearance of a Mr. John Ormond."

With that, the major dismissed the other agents and ushered the leader towards his parked car.

"Are you going to let them walk away, just like that?" the detective asked, in surprise. "Aren't you going to arrest them?"

"On what charge?" the other replied. "For failure to relieve you of *The Tarkov Papers*?"

It was a gratifying experience for George Mason to sit face-to-face with his bested adversary in Forsenius's office. Failing the re-surfacing of John Ormond, this turn of events, together with recovery of the missing manuscript, justified all his efforts of recent days and his constant tramping through the snowbound streets of the Finnish capital. There had been compensations, too, in the friendship and hospitality of the Kilpinens, the novel experience of the sauna and other aspects of Finnish life. *The Tarkov Papers* were now safely locked in the major's filing cabinet.

"Do you wish to make contact with your embassy?" Forsenius asked the Russian, as a matter of courtesy.

"I don't think that will be necessary at this stage," Maxim confidently replied. "Unless I am to be charged with something?"

He was a tall, athletically-built man of, Mason estimated, about forty years old. His brief movements were lithe and supple, those of a professional dancer; his eyes intelligent and alert.

"We cannot formally charge you with anything, unfortunately," Forsenius said, wary of creating an international incident, "since we have no evidence of any crime you have committed on Finnish soil. Just tell us what you know of the disappearance of John Ormond and we'll overlook your wasting valuable police time"

At mention of the translator's name, Maxim's taut features registered a half-smile. He shifted his position nervously and lit a cigarette.

"And if I don't co-operate?" he countered, evasively.

"We can take certain steps against you, short of formal charges," the major threatened. "One of which would be to ensure that your touring troupe, the Vladimir Dance Ensemble, would never again obtain clearance to perform in Finland."

Maxim's eyes narrowed perceptibly. Obviously ill-at-ease, he shifted his position again and said:

"There is nothing to relate. We are as much in the dark as you are regarding Mr. Ormond."

"You seemed pretty certain of his whereabouts," Mason objected, "when you sent us on that wild snow goose chase to Siltasaari."

Maxim's features broke into a wide grin.

"That was merely a ruse to throw you off the scent. Since you are now in possession of the property I was really after, something my superiors in Moscow were hell-bent on recovering, everything else, including the fate of John Ormond, is purely incidental."

"Do you deny that you met him on your previous tour in the spring?" Mason asked.

"Absolutely not," Maxim replied. "I did meet John Ormond and, what is more, I took to him at once. He spoke very passable Russian and was evidently much interested in our culture and way of life; unusually so for a Westerner."

"Where exactly did you meet?"

"At the Havis Club on Annankatu, where he attended our performance. He translated our publicity and, to thank him, I invited him to lunch at the Alphonse, a small French restaurant."

Mason smiled wryly at mention of the Havis, but did not refer to the phone calls his adversary had made, that had so unnerved him at the time.

"What sort of things did you discuss over lunch?" he asked instead.

"Russian authors mainly."

"Including Timor Tarkov?"

"Among several others," Maxim replied. "I in fact gave him a copy of Sholokov's *Tikii Don*, as a mark of my appreciation."

"Which you obtained at the Academic Bookshop, right here in Helsinki."

Maxim slowly nodded, regarding Mason with increased admiration and respect.

"You've obviously been doing your homework," he remarked.

"Keen as mustard, the Scotland Yard Special Branch," Forsenius put in, admiringly. "The Inspector here is one of their key men."

"That is certainly something I can appreciate," the Russian admitted, grudgingly "I have to admit, you were at least one step ahead of me, regrettably, all the way."

"Did you meet Ormond again after taking him to lunch?" Mason asked.

"That was the last I saw of him," Maxim replied.

"Your visa expires at the end of this year," the major said. "We expect you to be out of the country by that date. After some photographs for our files, you are free to leave."

"Can we take him at his word?" Mason asked, as Maxim exited with the duty officer.

"No other choice, really," the Finn replied. "Tell me, how did you latch on to the manuscript?"

"It was you yourself who led me to it," the detective replied. "The decimal point put an entirely new complexion on things."

"And how was that?" the major asked, still mystified.

"From something Paavo Kilpinen said about barrels of apples, it immediately suggested to me the Dewey Classification System. From there it was quite a short step, with deductive reasoning and *pace* the Estonian Trade Delegation, to the University Reference Library."

"Barrels of apples?" the Finn asked, dumbfounded. "Estonian Trade Delegation?"

"You now have the Tarkov manuscript safely secured in your filing cabinet," Mason said, with finality. "Let's just leave it at that."

"I suppose you will very shortly be leaving us," Forsenius then said, with genuine regret. "I've very much enjoyed my association with you."

"The feeling's mutual," the detective said warmly, heaving his portly frame out of the comfortable swivel-chair and stepping towards the door. "I leave in two days' time. That's the earliest I could book a flight in the run-up to Christmas."

"Give me a call before you leave. Just to say good-bye."

"If you're ever in London," Mason said, in parting, "get in touch. Adele and I would be delighted to show you round."

"I'll do that," Forsenius said, with a vigorous handshake.

On leaving Police Headquarters, George Mason walked in a contented frame of mind the length of Esplanade as far as the Swedish Theater and crossed the main thoroughfare to get a late lunch at The Three Counts. It had been quite a hectic morning's work and he felt he could do justice to a reindeer steak, served with boiled potatoes and red whortleberries, a staple of the lunch-hour menu. As he ate, he scanned the pages of *Helsingin Sanomat* to try and catch up as best he could on the latest international news, on events that had been unfolding while his attention had mainly been elsewhere. One photograph on the inside pages soon caught his eye. It showed the new British ambassador, Sir Parker Tate, in plus-fours and a deer-stalker hat, setting out on an elk-hunting expedition. It cheered him somehow to be reminded of home, even while feeling that some people had all the luck. The diplomatic service, he mused. Why had he never put in for it himself, if this was typical of the perks?

He spent an agreeable hour or so in this manner, deciphering the captions beneath the photographs and observing the bustle of activity along Mannerheim from the large picture-windows, before leaving the restaurant, dodging the trams and proceeding along Mikonkatu to collect a present for Adele from one of the station boutiques. As he drew near the entrance to the Polyglot Institute, he noticed from the other side of this narrow street of mainly commercial buildings something which made him duck quickly for cover inside a shop doorway. Unmistakably, he spotted the tall, bearded figure of Maxim Ivanovich just as he was leaving the Institute premises and watched him climb into a parked Vokswagen and slowly drive past him, heading towards Esplanade. Continuing on his way as soon as the coast was clear, he smiled ruefully to himself. Even though it may be of little practical importance at this stage, at least it confirmed something he had long suspected, that Arthur Greenwood, using the cover of a well-established language school, was heavily implicated in this affair and that his instinct not to trust him had been right all along.

CHAPTER THIRTEEN

G EORGE MASON AWOKE early on the day of his departure, despite spending a long, pleasant evening in the company of Virpi at the Havis Club, preceded by a farewell visit to the sauna at the Hotel Kivi and lengthy telephone calls to his wife Adele, to the Kilpinens and to Chief Inspector Harrington. He packed his suitcase neatly and ordered room service for a light breakfast, debating with himself whether he should inform Viljo Forsenius of Maxim's contact two days ago with Arthur Greenwood; or whether he should just leave things as they were and let sleeping dogs lie. He was pre-empted by the major himself, who placed a call to his room just as he had finished dressing.

"Good morning, Inspector Mason," came the up-beat voice of the Finn. "I hope you slept well?"

"Like a top, thank you," the detective replied.

"What time is your flight to London?"

"2 pm, from Seutola."

"Then get over here as quickly as you can. You have enough time. I have a surprise for you."

With that, he rang off and Mason fell to wondering what on earth he meant, as he carried his suitcase down to the hotel lobby to be held for him at reception and handed in his room keys. The thought crossed his mind, optimistically, that he might be in line for some sort of presentation for his detective work. Perhaps the Finnish Ministry of Culture was offering a cash reward, or possibly a medal of some description with which to impress Harrington and his colleagues at Scotland Yard. Nothing, however, could have prepared him in advance for what lay in store, as the Number 3 circular tram dropped him at South Harbor and he strode across the market square towards Police Headquarters.

As he was ushered by the duty officer into the major's office he saw a young man of medium build, with tousled blond hair, clad in a light anorak and slacks, sitting in the chair facing Forsenius's desk. Even without introductions, he knew at once who this was. Both men rose to their feet at the detective's entrance.

"Inspector Mason." Forsenius said, jubilantly, "let me introduce John Ormond. John, this is George Mason, all the way from London on special assignment to investigate your case."

The young man sprang forward to shake Mason's hand warmly.

"Delighted to meet you," he said. "And my heart-felt congratulations that you recovered the manuscript."

"He stole it from under the very noses of the KGB," the Finn said, enthusiastically. "One of their top agents, known as the Lynx, was assigned to it."

"You went to Tallinn, am I right?" Mason asked, addressing Ormond.

"You were right on the ball again, Inspector," Forsenius said, almost beside himself with admiration at the detective's acuity. "Tell him the full story, John."

"How on earth did you discover that?" asked the translator.

"By deductive logic," Mason replied, matter-of-factly.

"No flies on Scotland Yard Special Branch," the major remarked. "He pursued every possible line of enquiry, even the least promising."

Mason felt glad and relieved that his opposite number, to spare his blushes, made no reference to the defection theory he had originally strongly proposed.

"My story," Ormond said, "is quite simple, in a way. I did in fact book a trip, as you rightly surmised, to Tallinn at the end of April."

"For vacation purposes?"

"Actually no. There was an urgent practical reason. It was more a precautionary measure. About the same time I received the translation assignment of *The Tarkov Papers* from Paavo Kilpinen, I met a Russian dancer engaged at the Havis Club. We struck up an acquaintance in the club bar after the show and he invited me out to lunch to show his appreciation of the work I did on his program. I accepted, mainly because it seemed a good opportunity to practice my Russian."

"You are referring to Maxim Ivanovich Slovotkin." Mason interjected.

The young man slowly nodded agreement, his eyes registering both surprise and admiration.

"In the course of the meal we discussed Russian authors and he in fact gave me a signed copy of a well-known novel. When he turned the conversation repeatedly to Academician Tarkov and his various writings, I grew a little uneasy and suspicious. I felt he might be cultivating me in some way, to serve his own purposes."

"He could not have known for certain you had the manuscript," Forsenius put in. "He was probably on a fishing expedition."

"A short time before that," Ormond explained, "I received a telephone call from Tarkov himself in Switzerland. He offered me his encouragement on the difficult task ahead. He also mentioned that the Russian secret service would do their utmost to retrieve it, and that I was to be on my guard constantly."

"So you began to connect Maxim with the KGB?" Mason asked.

"Not in any definite sense, no. To me, he was just an outgoing artiste. He told me that his engagement in Helsinki lasted until May 3rd. Mainly out of general caution, but also because I had often wanted to visit Estonia, I decided on the spur of the moment to take a short trip to Tallinn, with the intention of returning May 4th, by which date the Vladimir Dance Ensemble would have returned to Leningrad."

"That was quite a long weekend," Mason remarked. "Somewhat over seven months."

Ormond smiled, rather sheepishly.

"Things did not turn out quite as I had anticipated," he replied.

"You're not going to believe this, Inspector," Forsenius put in. "Tell him, John, what you have just related to me. In a way, I feel responsible."

"You!" exclaimed the detective, in disbelief.

The young translator got up and paced the room, ran his hand through his tousled hair. From the window, gazing out across the harbor, he said with his back towards them:

"I got myself arrested."

"How on earth did you manage that?" Mason demanded, incredulously.

"It was a case of mistaken identity," Ormond replied, ruefully. "I happened to be carrying with me quite a large amount in American dollars, left over from a visit I made to New England last fall. The Estonian authorities had apparently recently received a tip-off from the Finnish police about an Englishman living in Finland who was smuggling currency across the Baltic. They were evidently on the look-out for someone carrying a British passport. They stopped me and did a search. The upshot was that they refused to accept my explanation about the dollars."

"It would have been our Anti-fraud Squad," Forsenius said, apologetically. "They handle money laundering, currency smuggling, stolen artworks and so forth."

"So you spent seven months as the guest of the Estonian state?"

"At a prison on the outskirts of Tallinn. The conditions were fairly rudimentary, but the food wasn't too bad and they treated me well enough on the whole. Allowed me access to a library and a gymnasium. The British Embassy were providing legal assistance. I was mainly concerned about the safety of the manuscript, which I had concealed at the University Reference Library."

"And which the Inspector was astute enough to discover, ahead of the KGB," Forsenius said.

"A very good thing that you did," Ormond said. "Paavo Kilpinen will be extremely relieved."

"So how did you manage to get out?" Mason asked.

"Eventually, they collared the real suspect trying to smuggle a briefcase full of high-denomination Deutschmark bills through Customs. He was an employee of a tour company based in Turku who made regular trips across the Baltic. Charges against me were dropped and I returned by ferry yesterday morning, going straight to the university. When I found that the manuscript was no longer there, I came here to report the theft to the police."

Major Forsenius crossed to his filing cabinet, took out the Manila package and handed it to the young translator.

"You have time to make up," he observed, wryly. "Timor Tarkov has been ringing almost daily."

"If I were you," Mason cautioned, "I would not say anything about this project to Arthur Greenwood at the Polyglot Institute."

Both Forsenius and Ormond looked at him questioningly.

"I have never trusted him," the detective said. "After our meeting here two days ago, I spotted Maxim Ivanovich leaving Greenwood's premises on Mikonkatu."

"So they are most likely in league," the major said, in some surprise.

"I'd cancel his residence permit, if I were you," Mason proposed.

"We'll certainly give the matter some serious thought," the other promised, making notes.

"My contract of employment with Greenwood terminates at the end of this year," Ormond explained. "It is renewable, but I have a standing invitation to teach translation at the Lahti Interpreters School, and I also need a new place to live. My apartment on Kulosaari has been re-let."

"Your effects have been placed in storage at the central police depot," Forsenius explained.

"The Kilpinens have offered to accommodate me over Christmas, until the New Year," Ormond then said. "After that, I shall transfer to Lahti and get down to serious work."

"Someone by the name of Helvi will be very pleased to see you again," Mason remarked.

The young man flushed slightly, tucked the Manila envelope securely under his arm and said:

"I'm going round there this very evening, soon as she finishes work."

"The Kilpinens were both very instrumental in recovering the goods," Mason said. "I would not have succeeded without them."

"Barrels of apples again, Inspector Mason?" Forsenius jibed, warmly shaking hands with his two visitors as they were on the point of leaving his office.

"Something of the sort," Mason replied, humorously.

"Then good-bye, and the very best of luck. Don't forget to keep in touch."